In The Bayous

A Jack Rabbit Adventure

M. L. Hollinger

White Glove Fiction™
1103 Middlecreek
Friendswood, Texas 77546
281-992-3131 Tel
www.WhiteGloveFiction.com

Copyright © 2022 by: M. L. Hollinger
Edited by: Jessica Tate
All rights reserved

ISBN: 978-1-64883-1423
UPC: 6-43977-41423-6

FIRST EDITION
1 2 3 4 5 6 7 8 9 10

To all of my old sci-fi pals.

About the Author

James Thompson is a retired Air Force officer with a vivid imagination. He's been writing since grade school, but only began a serious attempt at novels and short stories after fully retiring in 2001. Science fiction is a natural genre for him, stemming from eleven years' work on the military space program and serving as liaison officer with NASA on the Space Shuttle program. He is now fully retired and writing adventures like he is living them.

About the book

The Great Spirit assigns Jack his first adventure as a human being. His task is to save a teenaged boy from going down the wrong path in life.

Not only is Jack human for the first time, he is also a female for the first time. This new shape is puzzling to him, but the Great Spirit helps him adjust.

Will he succeed? How will he turn his boy away from delinquency? Jack must use all his powers in performing the task set before him.

In the process, he learns how to hunt alligators and cook southern fried chicken as well as how to behave like a human instead of a rabbit.

You will laugh and cry as you follow Jack's actions in this unique adventure.

M. L. Hollinger

Introduction

It was a great morning, bright, hot and sunny in the west Texas hill country. Jack Rabbit was awake and moving from his burrow, ready for breakfast. He was in the mood for some fresh sprouts and knew where they were growing, up the mountain side. Jack weaved around the cactus and sage brush starting up the well know path to higher ground. After a few minutes of travel, he stopped wondering at a new noise. Moving slow, he hopped closer. From behind a giant red barrel cactus he nosed around for a peek. To Jack's surprise, an Apache medicine man was chanting and dancing around a small fire. The medicine man was dressed in feathers with his body painted in many colors. Most noticeable was his left hand, it was painted all white up to his wrist like a glove. In his right hand he held what looked like a ball of bones, sticks, feathers, cloth, and who knows what else wrapped around what resembled a skull.

Jack heard a small crack and looked up the mountain side. A small puff of dust spit out into the sun shine. Jack had seen rock slides before but this was different. He noticed one big rock beginning to move. He was directly in the path of the rock and jumped sideways as rabbits do then started to run. He let out a loud screech bolting past the dancing medicine man, shocking him out of the trance. The shaman fell backwards into a crevice in the mountain side.

Jack joined him in the narrow opening to get away from the boulder. Both Jack and the shaman watched a very large rock land on the trail and fall over the side of the cliff. Needless to say, Jack had saved the shaman's life.

The shaman looked down at Jack. "Wow that was close. Thank you for saving my life."

"What is your name?" the shaman asked. "Jack Rabbit," replied the rabbit. "Hello Jack, my name is Mohan. I am the medicine man for my Apache tribe."

"How do you speak my language," asked Jack. "How can I understand you?"

"The Great Spirit has impowered me with great wisdom and the ability perform many wonderous tasks. May I ask you what you desire most?"

Jack knew immediately what he wanted to be. "Currently my life is short in comparison to yours. I wish to be many things, go many places and have a very long life."

Mohan went back outside and rebuilt the fire. Jack stayed in the crevice away from danger. Once the fire was just the right size, Mohan went way back into the dark crevice mumbling words Jack could not understand. He could hear Mohan moving around taping and scraping in the dark. He jumped as Mohan let out a loud "Ah Ha! Found it," and came shuffling out of the narrow passage. Back to the fire went the Shaman. He opened his medicine bag, pulled out several items and began to chant, repeating a rhythmic phrase and dancing around the fire. After a few minutes he called for Jack to come out of the crevice.

Cautiously, Jack stepped close to Mohan, staying away from the cliff side and the fire. He was afraid to be too close to the fire because his fur could burn.

Mohan, still chanting and dancing, threw something into the fire which exploded with a bright flash. Jack jumped back close to the mountain wall. Mohan laughed and coached him back to his spot. He asked Jack to move onto the top of a rock he placed next to the fire.

Jack was hesitant but decided he would be safe with Mohan. He seemed nice and had a good voice for chanting.

Mohan suddenly stopped in front of Jack and threw a dust ball toward Jack. Jack's face and both ears were filled with the powder, and it covered him from his head down to his lucky feet.

Rabbits have lucky feet, you know.

Mohan started to chant and dance again. Jack began to sway back and forth in response to Mohan's hypnotic voice.

Magical powers swirled around them. Sparks flew from the fire, clouds rolled in, lightning lit up the sky, rocks crashed down the mountain, thunder rolled through the valley, cactus burst into flower, grass turned green, water sprung from the crevice to form a small creek flowing down the side of the mountain, a star fell, and Jack passed out.

Jack woke up feeling a little strange. Looking around he saw Mohan sleeping on the ground next to the dying fire. Getting up he went to the creek to get a drink. The water was the sweetest he had ever tasted. Looking around he spotted some fresh green sprouts which were tender and tasted really awesome. He hopped over to the sleeping Mohan who was just waking up.

"What just happened?" asked Jack.

Mohan sat up and stretched. "Well Jack," he said, "you are now a very special being. You have many powers to experiment with. First test your abilities. Picture in you mind that you are an Apache warrior."

Jack thought "I am an Apache warrior." The air stood still, a little fire flashed before his eyes, a wind blew some dust into his face, producing a tear.

Mohan said, "Jack go look at your face in the stream." Moving to the stream Jack looked into the standing pool and saw an Apache warrior looking back at him. "Mohan," he cried "what is going on?"

Mohan laughed a little and said, "Jack, you are now what we call a cambiante, a changeling. A cambiante is a being with many powers. He can become any being he wishes to be. The Great Spirit has also granted you never ending life. You have the power of time. You can venture to the past or future. There is only one catch to this magical existence you will be living. You can do no harm to others except when someone bad is harming others. Your life is now designed to be helpful to all beings everywhere you go. Protect the innocent from the bad people."

Mohan paused, "Jack there are however some restrictions. First, you must go wherever the Great Spirit bids you go."

"That sounds reasonable," Jack says. "Is there anything else?"

"You may also never visit Easter Island as the awful 'Z Gods' there will harm you. And one more thing you can never eat papaya fruit."

"Papaya fruit, what is that," Jack thought.

Over the next weeks and months Jack changed from one character to another, Panther, Eagle, mouse, etc. "This is going to be fun," Jack thought.

Jack wondered over the Apache territory for many years changing as he saw fit. He really liked being a bird. Birds could see a lot of things on the ground, fly fast and travel long distances. Jack liked being ground animals, Panthers were his choice. Most of all Jack liked being human even if he could be a big tree or a small bush just to watch the world go by.

He waited for the Great Spirit's call and wondered what his first assignment would be.

Chapter 1

I'm certainly not in Texas anymore. I peruse my surroundings. Instead of the plains outside El Paso I'm surrounded by Cypress trees with roots deep in swamp water. The oppressive heat doesn't stop the mosquitos from biting, and I slap at one buzzing close to my ear. I'm on dry land, but the stench of the rotting vegetation wafts in on a foul breeze.

The swamp sounds are soon eclipsed by the roar of an engine and the noise of a propellor torturing the air. An airboat soon comes into sight skimming gracefully over the grass to my left. The driver is a husky black man in denim shorts and a flannel shirt with the sleeves cut off. Two dead gators line the bottom of his hull.

"Hey honey, what you doin' out in the middle o' nowhere all alone?" he shouts over the engine noise.

What does he mean by 'honey' Great Spirit?

YOU ARE A FEMALE.

I look at my arms and hands and see dark skin and a slender shape not at all like the jack rabbit reflection in the small pond I was drinking at yesterday. What the...? Further inspection reveals a print cotton dress and large black bare feet at the end of slender legs. I suddenly realize what's happened.

The Great Spirit has done this. This must be my first human assignment. Better come up with a good story for this guy.

"I ran away, an' I got nowhere ta go." *That's a good first line, and I thought of it all by myself.*

The engine stops, and the driver leans toward me. "Can you handle a rifle?" he asks.

I can do anything if the Great Spirit will help me, but he doesn't know that. I'm a female now which means I'm supposed to be delicate, but I guess I'm not too delicate or I wouldn't have run away.

"I think so. My Daddy used to let me shoot his shotgun."

He lifts a rifle from under his seat and hands it to me. "This is an M1 carbine. It's automatic. All you gots to do is point it and pull th' trigger. Can you do that?"

I've seen hunters handle these things. I know which end is dangerous, and I know to point it at something that's not alive.

"Like this?" I raise the rifle to my shoulder and point it at a Cypress knee then pull the trigger. Nothing happens. The man begins to laugh.

"I forgot to tell you to take off the safety." He shows me the safety.

This time, a round slams into the cypress knee.

The big man applauds and takes back the rifle. "Okay, you can help me out. I needs t' fill two more tags 'fore I gotta git home to my boy. Get aboard."

He helps me into the air boat and says, "My name's Moline Thibodeaux, but everybody calls me Gator. What's your name?"

Okay, what do I say? The only name I know is Jack Rabbit, but that isn't a girl's name. I know, "It's Jaqueen, Jaqueen Rabitte."

He starts the engine, and we pull out into the bayou. "Pretty name. I like Jaqueen."

He points to the dead gators. "See where I shot 'em?"

I look at the carcasses and notice the bullet holes. "Um hum."

"When I pulls those gators upside the boat, you shoots 'em right there. Got it?"

"Um hum, I gots it."

He laughs again as we pull up next to a cypress branch with a steel wire stretched into the water.

"Looks like I got me a good sized one here," he says.

He begins to haul in the wire, and I soon see a very large gator attached to it. It begins to thrash about wildly as it nears the surface.

"Git that rifle ready!" he shouts.

I pick up the rifle and flip off the safety then stand ready to shoot. Moline maneuvers the gator so I can get a good shot at the spot I noticed on the other kills. I pull the trigger, and the gator stops thrashing.

"Good girl! You did good, child." He hauls the gator aboard and removes the large hook from its mouth before baiting it again with a chicken carcass. He crimps a plastic tag to the tail of his gator and arranges it with the others before starting the engine again.

The next two hooks are bare and need rebaiting, but the third yields a medium-sized prize.

Moline shades his eyes and looks toward the sun. "Gittin' late. You wanna go back home?"

"Huh uh, I aint never goin' back there ever agin." This has to be my assignment, and I need to stay close. I can only hope he asks me to come with him.

"Can ya cook?" he asks.

Now here's a problem. If I say no, he'll probably take me to the police. All I can hope for is the Great Spirit will give me the knowledge. Can I cook?

I WILL GUIDE YOU. TELL HIM YOU'RE A GOOD COOK.

"Sho I kin. I cook fo my Daddy an' my brothers all the time."

"Okay, you kin come to my place fo a while. I'm tired o' cookin'."

The air boat skims over the bayous for several minutes then pulls up to a small-town dock. A middle-aged white lady in overalls walks from a small pole barn to greet Moline.

"Hey Gator, what ya got for me?"

"I gots three gooduns an' a runt, Shirley."

Shirley inspects the gators and pays Moline from a pouch hanging from her waist. She summons two burly black men from the pole barn who unload her purchases. Moline bids her goodbye, and we're underway again. This time the destination is a small cabin on a large lake. Moline moors the air boat and leads me into the cabin.

"It aint much, but it's home," he says.

I've never been inside a human's house before. It's quite curious. They have so many different things inside, and I have no idea what they're for. I look around amazed.

TO YOUR LEFT IS A KITCHEN. THAT'S WHERE HUMANS PREPARE THEIR MEALS.

Prepare meals? Don't they just eat things like us animals?

NO, HUMANS COOK THEIR FOOD. THEY EAT SOME THINGS RAW, BUT MOSTLY THEY COOK. TO YOUR RIGHT IS WHAT THEY CALL A LIVING ROOM. THEY SIT THERE TO TALK AND WATCH TELEVISION.

Television?

YOU'LL SEE HOW THAT WORKS LATER.

The cabin looks clean and neatly arranged. A door in the back wall is closed.

What's behind that door?

THE BEDROOMS AND THE BATHROOM. HUMANS HAVE SPECIAL PLACES TO SLEEP AND RELIEVE THEMSELVES.

Why don't they just go outside and do it?

HUMANS DON'T DO THAT. YOU'LL HAVE TO LEARN TO USE THE BATHROOM. I'LL HELP YOU THERE.

Moline goes to a large white box and takes out a beer can. I've seen humans drink from those things before. I don't like them because they usually just throw them anywhere.

"Want a beer?" he asks.

BEER IS ALCOHOL. YOU ARE NOT PERMITTED ALCOHOL. ASK FOR SODA.

"No thanks. You got any soda?"

He produces another can and hands it to me. I watch as he opens his beer to see how I open my can. I follow his actions and the swoosh surprise me a bit, but I am thirsty. A tentative sip at the can produces a pleasant sensation in my mouth. I've never tasted anything like it. I down the whole can quickly.

"You musta bin thirsty, gal."

"I guess I was."

"Sit down and tell me somethin' 'bout yaself," he says as he takes a seat in a wooden rocking chair and motions toward a larger, softer thing.

Great Spirit, what do I know about how humans live? You must help me!

YOUR MOTHER ABANDONED YOU CHILDREN. YOU LIVE WITH YOUR FATHER, TWO BROTHERS AND TWO SISTERS. YOU ARE THE YOUNGEST. THEY EXPECT YOU TO DO ALL THE CHORES. YOUR FATHER BEATS YOU. YOU COULD TAKE NO MORE AND RAN AWAY.

I tell him that story, and he nods in understanding. "My Daddy used to beat the tar outta me. He blamed me for killin' mama cause she died birthin' me. I ran away too and made my own way."

He sits back in his chair and closes his eyes. A serene look spreads over his face. "I married a fine woman. We wuz so happy here in this cabin. Then Zach came along. We both loved him so much. Then, two years back she caught a fever and died. It hit me hard, but it near killed Zach. He aint been good since. He needs a woman's touch. That's why I brought you here." He sits up and looks me squarely in the eye. "I'm hopin' you can help him out. I've tried to talk to him, but I don't think I'm gettin' through to him."

I don't understand. What's wrong with his son? How could I help? I'm only a rabbit in human form. If we rabbits have a bad kit, the problem takes care of itself. It usually dies because of its bad habits.

HUMAN CHILDREN ARE NOT LEFT TO FEND FOR THEMSELVES. ADULTS, USUALLY THEIR PARENTS, TRY TO GUIDE THEM DOWN THE RIGHT PATH. HUMAN CHILDREN CAN BE QUITE OBSTINATE AND OFTEN EMBARK ON A PATH LEADING TO CRIME.

Crime? What is crime?

HUMANS HAVE LAWS THAT GOVERN THEIR BEHAVIOR.
A HUMAN WHO DOES NOT FOLLOW THEIR LAWS IS
PLACED IN A BUILDING CALLED A PRISON. OFTEN, THEY
ARE KEPT THERE FOR A VERY LONG TIME. SOME EVEN
DIE THERE.

What a strange idea. I'm glad we animals don't do that.
Maybe Zach has broken a law?

"Is Zach in trouble with the law?" I ask.

Moline sighs heavily. "Not yet, but he's hangin' out with
some punks who might get him in trouble. That's what worries
me."

YOU CAN HELP ZACH. TALK TO HIM.

"I'll talk to him. Maybe he'll listen to me."

"That'll be a miracle. He sure won't listen to me." Moline
rises from his chair and moves toward the door. "I got some
chores outside. You better check out the kitchen if'n you gonna
cook us some supper."

He walks out the door, and I move to the kitchen.

I don't know how to cook, Great Spirit.

I WILL HELP YOU. OPEN THE LARGE WHITE BOX. IT'S A
REFRIGERATOR. HUMANS KEEP FOOD IN IT.

I open the refrigerator thing and fall back in disgust. The
carcasses of two rabbits are the first things I see.

YES, HUMANS EAT RABBITS, BUT YOU KNOW THAT. GET
OVER IT.

Yes, sir, but why is it so cold in there?

THE COLD PRESERVES THE FOOD.

I find other items that look like food. One is a chicken carcass. I pick it up.

THAT'S A GOOD CHOICE. CUT IT UP AND FRY IT. I'LL TELL YOU HOW. PUT IT BACK FOR NOW. IT'S TOO EARLY TO START SUPPER.

As I'm putting the chicken back in the refrigerator, a tall teen-aged boy walks through the front door. He's a good-looking boy with a close haircut and lovely brown eyes. He looks at me with a startled expression.

"Who you?" he asks.

"I'm Jaqueen. You must be Zach."

"Yeah, you my Daddy's ho?"

A "HO" IS A WOMAN WHO HAS SEX FOR MONEY. YOU ARE NOT A "HO".

"No, I aint no ho. Yo Daddy took me in 'cause I run away from home. I gonna cook fo you an' yo Daddy and help him hunt gators."

"I sho hope you kin cook. Daddy don't do so good with cookin'."

I know I've got lots of help in that job, and I'm going to need every bit of it. Humans sure have it rough having to cook their meals. Why can't they just eat things from nature, like rabbits?

"You gonna find out. I gonna cook fried chicken tonight."

A smile crosses Zach's face. "With biscuits an' gravy and greens?"

"Yes sir." Whatever all that is.

"Okay, I'll be back in plenty o' time fo dinnah."

HE NEEDS TO DO HIS HOMEWORK.

What's homework?

HUMANS ARE TAUGHT IN BUILDINGS CALLED SCHOOLS. THEY ARE ASSIGNED WORK TO DO AT HOME TO PREPARE FOR THE NEXT DAY'S LESSON. IT'S CALLED HOMEWORK, AND HE NEEDS TO DO IT BEFORE HE GOES OUT.

He starts for the door, but I call to him, "Whoa there. Aint you got homework?"

"I does that after dinner," he says, then he turns toward the door again just as Moline opens it.

"You goin' someplace, son?"

Zach backs off and takes on a contrite expression. "I got a ballgame back at school."

"Ball game, or hangin' out with that bunch of thugs you call friends?"

"Ball game, Daddy, honest."

"Well, it can wait 'til you finish your homework. Now, get busy."

The look on Moline's face and his hulking stance tell me he's ready to back up his order with force if necessary. Zach gets the message and moves to the kitchen table picking up the thing he wore on his back when he came in.

THAT'S CALLED A BACKPACK. SCHOOL CHILDREN KEEP THEIR BOOKS, THEIR LUNCH AND A FEW OTHER THINGS IN IT.

Moline leaves the house again after taking a shotgun down from a rack beside the door and pocketing a handful of shells. "I'm goin' huntin'. Be back in time for supper." He walks out the door leaving me alone with Zach.

I decided not to disturb the boy and busy myself with supper. The Great Spirit guides me through the process. I can't help but feel sorry for the poor chicken as I dismembered it. I wonder how it will taste cooked. I'd stolen a chicken once when I was an eagle, and it wasn't bad raw.

The greens should be easy. I guess the humans eat them just like we rabbits do, but the Great Spirit steps in.

YOU COOK THE GREENS TOO. IN THAT CUPBOARD BY YOUR KNEE, YOU'LL FIND A POT.

I open the small door and see several metal things. Are those pots?

YES, TAKE THE TOP ONE AND FILL IT HALF FULL OF WATER.

I pick up the pot and start to go out to the lake.

NO, USE THE FAUCET THERE IN FRONT OF YOU.

I set the pot down and stare at the shiny things in back of the steel basin.

THAT'S A SINK. THE WATER CONTROLS ARE IN THE BACK. THE HANDLE ON THE RIGHT IS COLD WATER. JUST TURN IT.

I turn the handle and water flows out of a spout. That's wonderful. Humans have water at their command.

YES, THE HANDLE ON THE LEFT IS HOT WATER. USE

THAT TO WASH THE DISHES.

I turn that handle and the water gets warm. I turn off the cold handle and the water soon gets too hot to touch. Even more wonderful. What don't these humans have?

PUT THE POT ON THE STOVE AFTER YOU PUT IN THE WATER.

Where's a 'stove'?

IT'S TO YOUR LEFT. NOTICE THERE ARE FOUR PLACES TO PUT THE POT. PUT IT ON ONE OF THE LARGER ONES.

I do as the Great Spirit says and step back. Does it 'cook' now?

NO, YOU HAVE TO TURN ON THE BURNER. SEE THE KNOBS?

I figure out the burner operation, and the Great Spirit tells me to add the greens after washing the grit out of the leaves. The biscuits are a little harder. I have to learn the oven. Great Spirit tells me the gravy will come later.

Zach stays busy with his homework until he asks me, "What's the square root of 169?"

I look at him and shake my head. "Lord, don't ask me, child. I don't know nothin' 'bout numbers. What's a 'square root'?"

He laughs softly but explains, "A square's a number multiplied by itself. Th' number you use is th' square root o' that number."

Now rabbits don't do math even though I've heard humans say we multiply quickly. The Great Spirit supplies the answer.

THE ANSWER IS 13, BUT MAKE HIM FIGURE IT OUT.

I think for a moment and look at my fingers. Two fingers and two more makes four. Two must be the square root of four. "Okay, what's two times two?"

"Four. Everybody know th' square root o' four be two."

"Okay, go up from there. What's three times three?"

"Everybody knows that one too."

"So, keep usin' bigger numbers 'til you gets 169."

A smile creeps over his face as he scribbles on another piece of paper. "Ten times ten's a hundred. Leben times leben is…121. Twelve times twelve is … 144. Thirteen times thirteen … is 169. That's cool Jaqueen."

'COOL' IS A TEEN WORD MEANING GOOD, SUPER, CLEVER OR ADMIRABLE.

I figure it's a compliment. "Thanks."

Zach finishes his homework just as Moline comes in with two more rabbits. He hangs the shotgun back on the rack.

"I'm gonna dress these here rabbits. I figured we'd need more'n two with you part o' th' house now."

I don't know if I can bear to eat rabbit. I didn't eat them when I was an eagle, but I thank him anyway.

"Can I go play ball now Daddy? My homework's all done." Zach asks.

"How soon to supper?" Moline asks me.

THE BISCUITS WILL ONLY TAKE ANOTHER TEN MINUTES AND YOU CAN DO THE GRAVY NOW. TELL HIM FIFTEEN MINUTES.

"Supper'll be ready in fifteen minutes," I say.

"You heard Jaqueen. Go wash up and help set th' table," Moline commands his son.

Over supper I turn the conversation to a subject of my own curiosity. I know many human names, but I've never heard Moline.

"How come they calls you Moline?" I ask.

Zach can't help but giggle. Moline gives him a stern look.

"My Daddy seen a guy drivin' a tractor inta town one day and liked the name on the tractor. My Mama was carryin' me at th' time, an' he told her if I was a boy, that'd be my name."

It made sense to me, but Zach could hardly control his mirth.

"You shouldn't laugh at yo Daddy's name, child," I scold him.

"I can't help it. I get ragged about it at school all the time."

I've seen tractors in the fields. They're powerful things, and Moline's a big man.

"You just tell 'em your Daddy's built like one o' them tractors, and nobody messes with him."

"Where'd you learn to fry chicken this good? It's downright divine." Moline asks.

"You might say I had some divine help," I answer.

"You what?"

"I mean, I gotta thank my sainted Mother up in heaven for teachin' me." Whew, I almost gave myself away there.

"Can I go play ball now, Daddy? My homework's all done."

"You be home before nine, hear. I don't want you runnin' 'round with those thugs after dark."

"They aint thugs, they's my bros."

"Bros, eh? Stay with that crowd, and you'll be 'bros' in prison."

"Okay, can I go?"

"Yeah, go ahead."

After he leaves, Moline helps me with the dishes, and I

question him about Zach.

"How he do in school?"

"He do okay. He a bright kid, but he done taken up with a bad bunch after school. I'm really worried about him."

ASK HIM ABOUT WHAT ZACH LIKES TO DO BESIDES SCHOOL.

"What he like 'sides school?"

Moline huffs an answer, "Nothin'. Nothin' besides hangin' out with those thugs."

ASK ABOUT SPORTS.

"Do he like sports?"

"He likes basketball, and he could make the school team if he'd go out for it, but he don't think that's 'cool'."

We finish the dishes, and Moline brings up the subject of sleeping arrangements. It is getting dark, and I agree it's time for sleep. Moline moves to the wall and touches a small panel. The room suddenly becomes bright.

DON'T BE AFRAID. YOU'VE SEEN LIGHTS IN HUMAN HOUSES BEFORE. THEY HAVE WHAT'S CALLED ELECTRICITY. IT ALSO RUNS THE REFRIGERATOR AND THE STOVE.

I relax now that I know how humans get the lights I've seen through their windows. Moline continues, "We only got two places to sleep. One's mine and one's Zach's, but you can sleep here on the couch if you want."

I think about that for a moment and decide a nearby tree would be better. "I'll just sleep outside, I think."

Moline looks at me with a puzzled expression.   "The skeeters'll eat you 'live."

"They don't bother me none. I'll be just fine."

He shrugs his shoulders, "Your funeral, but you come inside if it gets too bad, hear?"

"Don't worry 'bout me."

He stretches and yawns, "I think I'll go to bed early. I got more gator tags to fill, and I wanna get an early start in the mornin'. Goodnight."

"Goodnight. See ya in th' mornin'."

He goes off to the bedroom, and I slip out the door. I know the skeeters are bad, so I turn into a gator and slip into the water. I keep an eye on the cabin to watch for Zach.

I don't know how long I floated there, but I'm sure Zach is much later than his father's curfew time. He goes into the house, and I quickly change back to Jaqueen and follow him in.

"I think you late," I say.

He turns with a surprised look. "I didn't see you outside."

"I didn't want you to see me. How come you so late?"

"The game went longer'n I spected, that's all."

HE'S LYING. HE'S BEEN SMOKING POT.

Pot? What's pot?

IT'S LIKE CATNIP FOR HUMANS, BUT IT'S ILLEGAL YOU SHOULD SCOLD HIM FOR DOING IT. TELL HIM YOU CAN SMELL IT.

"Why do I smell pot on you, then?"

"We was just playin' ball. I didn't smoke no pot."

"Don't lie to me. I got a nose like a hound dog, and I know pot when I smells it."

He takes on a contrite expression and lowers his head. "It was just one joint."

A JOINT IS A CIGARETTE MADE WITH MARAJUANA. IT IS THE FIRST STEP IN DRUG ADDICTION. THEY'LL GROW TIRED OF THAT SOON AND GO TO HARD DRUGS TO GET HIGH.

I shake my head vehemently. "And I thought you was a smart boy. Don't you know the next thing you'll want is somethin' stronger?"

"I won't do that. I won't do no hard drugs."

"Did you wanna do pot?"

He turns his head away from me and frowns. "No, but Darrell said it was cool and everybody does it."

"I don't. Your Daddy don't. We don't want to. We don't need it ta be 'cool', and you don't neither."

"They's my bros. How can I say no to them?"

"Maybe you needs some different bros?"

"They's the coolest bros at school."

"What? You got no basketball team, no football team?"

"They's jock straps, they aint cool." He snorts in disgust.

HIGH SCHOOL ATHLETES ARE ADMIRED BY MOST STUDENTS, BUT THE DELINQUENTS DENIGRATE THEM. ATHLETES CAN GET COLLEGE SCHOLARSHIPS FOR A FREE EDUCATION.

"Why, 'cause Darrell say so? Some o' those 'jock straps' are gonna get ta go t' college. You gonna go t' college?"

"We can't 'ford no college."

I point to the couch. "Sit down, Zach. We gotta talk."

"Can we do this some other time? I'm tired, and I got school tomorrow."

"No, this won't take long. Sit down."

He plops onto the couch with a sour expression. "Another pep talk?" he asks.

I take the chair opposite him. "No, you gonna tell me somethin'."

He looks up surprised. "What's that?"

"What you wanna be after you finishes school?"

He looks at me with a thoughtful expression for a silent moment.

"I don't know."

"Look 'round you, boy. They must be somethin' you want 'sides bein' 'cool'. I aint talkin' 'bout next week. I mean when you a man."

"I know I don't wanna hunt gators. I wanna make good money and be rich."

"How you gonna do that with no education?"

He throws his head back and laughs. "Easy, Darrell makes lots o' money now. He got no more education than me."

HE MAKES MONEY SELLING DRUGS, WHICH IS ILLEGAL. HE WILL BE IN JAIL FOR A LONG TIME IN A FEW YEARS.

"And how long that good for?"

"Forever, I guess."

"How long afore the law catches up ta him?"

Zach laughs again. "He smarter'n any cop."

HE MAY ESCAPE THE LAW FOR A FEW YEARS, BUT HIS MAIN DANGER IS FROM OTHER DRUG DEALERS. MANY TIMES, THESE SMALL TIME DEALERS RUN INTO TROUBLE

WITH THEIR SUPPLIERS OR OTHER DRUG DEALERS. THEY
ARE RUTHLESS MEN WHO DO NOT BAULK AT MURDER.

"Is he smarter'n his supplier? What happen to him if he
makes him mad some way?"

Zach snorts a reply, "He know better'n that."

"Check it out and let me know how many Darrells make it
past five years in the business. I be interested to know."

"Can I go to bed now?" he asks.

"Go ahead. I told your Daddy I'm gonna sleep outside. I
think that's better'n messin' up th' sleepin' 'rangements.
Goodnight."

He goes to his room, and I go back outside where I take on the
form of an owl and roost in a nearby branch after a late snack of
wild mice.

Chapter 2

The next day at dawn, I change back to Jaqueen and begin fixing breakfast with the help of the Great Spirit. These humans require a lot of help just getting fed. I think I'm lucky to just find a patch of tender grass. Stealing the eggs from the hen house isn't easy. I apologize to each one as I take their babies away. The stuff they call bacon comes from pigs, I know, but someone else has to kill the hogs. Biscuits are easy for me now, but coffee takes some training time.

Zach is first out, dressed and ready for school.

"Mornin' Jaqueen. You sleep good outside last night?"

"I always sleeps good. Don't worry none 'bout me. How many eggs you want?"

"Just two, over easy."

THAT MEANS JUST TURN THEM OVER IN THE PAN ONCE THE WHITES ARE FIRM.

As I fry his eggs I ask, "You think any more 'bout what we talk 'bout last night?"

He wolfs down his orange juice before he answers. "No use thinkin' 'bout that. A man has t' be cool."

I drop the eggs on a plate and add some bacon and two biscuits. I set the plate in front of him. "Like I said, take a good look 'round and see if you see anything you'd like to be six, seben years from now. That's what 'cool' is."

He gulps down his breakfast and rises from the table. "See ya later."

He rushes out the door just as Moline is emerging sleepy-eyed and in pajama pants and bare chest.

"Take care, son," he calls to a slamming screen door. "You sleep okay?" he asks me.

"Yes, I did. I was fine outside. How many eggs you want?"

"Three, but where you sleep?"

"Don't you worry none 'bout that. I got lots o' places that's real comfortable."

He seems to accept that answer and drinks his juice while he waits for breakfast.

"You wanna hunt gators with me today?" he asks.

"Sure, I'll help."

"You need some other clothes? That dress aint too suited to huntin'."

"I aint got nothin' else even back home."

He eyes me up and down a moment. "I think some o' Zach's old clothes'd fit ya. I'll dig some out o' th' Goodwill pile after breakfast."

I join him for breakfast, and while I'm cleaning up, he vanishes back into the sleeping area and returns with a pair of well-worn jeans and a T-shirt with a high school logo.

"Try these on. You can change in the bathroom."

What's a bathroom?

IT'S WHERE HUMANS RELIEVE THEMSELVES. THEY DON'T JUST DO IT ANYLWHERE LIKE RABBITS. THROUGH THAT DOOR.

For the first time I see what's behind the door. Moline's bedroom is to the left, and Zach's is on the right. Neither bed is made. A small room dead ahead must be the 'bathroom'. It has an enclosure that seems to be wet.

THAT'S A SHOWER. HUMANS BATHE QUITE OFTEN. THEY
GO IN THERE AND TURN ON WATER WHICH FLOWS
FROM THAT FLOWER-LIKE DEVICE ON THE WALL.
YOU'LL NEED TO USE IT AFTER THE HUNT TODAY, AND
THEN EVERY OTHER DAY AFTER THAT. HUMANS DON'T
LIKE TO SMELL THEIR OWN SCENT.

A small basin sits against one wall with a mirror above it.

THAT'S A SINK. HUMANS USE IT TO WASH THEIR HANDS
AND BRUSH THEIR TEETH.

Another device is very strange to me. It has a lid and a box
sitting behind the lid.

THAT'S A TOILET. HUMANS USE IT FOR THEIR
URINATION AND DEFICATION. YOU WILL HAVE TO USE
IT WHILE YOU'RE HUMAN. LIFT THE LID.

I lift the lid and see a pool of water.

DON'T DRINK THAT WATER. THE WATER IN THE SINK IS
GOOD TO DRINK, BUT THIS WATER IS NOT GOOD FOR
HUMANS. YOU MAY DRINK IT WHEN YOU'RE AN
ANIMAL, BUT NOT NOW. IF YOU FEEL THE URGE, YOU SIT
ON THE SEAT AND GO.

I went this morning as an owl, but I do feel the need again. I
notice the lid is in two parts, and it appears the lower half is more
suitable as a seat, so, I put it down before I sit.

REMEMBER TO REMOVE YOUR CLOTHES BEFORE YOU GO.

That only seems logical, particularly since I plan to change. I remove my dress and the small pants under it before I sit.

When I'm finished, I rise and start to dress in the new clothes.

THE ROLL OF PAPER ON YOUR RIGHT IS USED TO CLEAN YOUR PRIVATE PARTS AFTER YOU GO.

I was wondering about that. As a rabbit, I just rub my bottom on the grass. I tear off a section of the paper and use it instead. I like it. It's much softer than grass.

NOW FLUSH. USE THE SILVER HANDLE ON THE BOX.

I push down on the handle, and recoil at the sudden rush of water.

Will it flood the room?

NO, IT WILL ONLY REFILL THE BOX.

I put on the T-shirt. It's a bit tight, but it fits. The jeans are a perfect fit.

What do I do with the dress?'

IT WILL NEED TO BE WASHED.

I pick it up and begin to lick it as I always did my fur.

NO, NO, HUMANS HAVE MACHINES THAT CLEAN CLOTHES. I'LL TEACH YOU ABOUT THAT LATER. JUST PUT IT ON THE FLOOR NEXT TO THE TOILET.

I leave the dress and rejoin Moline. He eyes me with a strange expression.

"Umm, umm what a difference clothes makes."

"What you mean?" I ask.

"Just sayin'. Come on, we got some gators t' catch."

We get our quota of gators, and Moline takes them into the village to collect his money. Then he surprises me.

"Come on, we gotta get you some clothes an' things," he says.

He leads me to a corner store where he picks out a few outfits, some underwear and a contraption he calls a bra. We finish it off with some canvas shoes and cotton stockings. I try it all on and feel so odd. But I guess since humans have no fur, they need something to cover their bare skin. Next, we go to another place where he buys something he calls a toothbrush and some things in jars and tubes.

THOSE THINGS ARE FOR YOUR PERSONAL USE. I'LL SHOW YOU HOW YOU USE THEM LATER.

It takes nearly half the money he got for the gators to buy my clothes and the other things.

"Moline, don't ya need that money for you an' Zach?" I say.

"We got food for a while, and I can hunt up food if we runs short. I just got tired o' lookin' at you in that feed sack dress."

We get back to the cabin in plenty of time before Zach is due home from school. Moline shows me where to put the things he bought for me, and I stack them in place.

"You want some lunch?" I ask.

"Why don't you fry up one o' those rabbits?" he says.

I cringe as I pull one of the stiff carcasses from the refrigerator. The Great Spirit helps me cut it up and cook the pieces. I serve it to him along with some left-over biscuits from breakfast. He takes a bottle of beer from the fridge and sits down at the kitchen table.

"Don't you want no rabbit?" he asks.

I turn my head away as he bites into a hind leg.

"No thanks, I aint hungry."

I see him spit out a tiny black ball, and it piques my curiosity.

"What's that you spit out?" I ask.

"Just some o' the shot from the shotgun shell."

HE SHOOTS THE RABBITS WITH A WEAPON CALLED A SHOTGUN. YOU'VE SEEN IT DONE BEFORE. IT SPRAYS A PATTERN OF LEAD SHOT. THAT'S WHAT YOU SEE HIM SPIT OUT.

I shudder at how my poor cousin died, but I understand why it must be so. Many animals live by killing and eating other animals. Humans are no exception to that rule, though they could eat only vegetables if they chose to. I think about the situation some more, and I decide that if Moline likes rabbit, I could save him the trouble of the lead shot by becoming an eagle and catching the rabbits that way.

"These are good swamp rabbits. Sure you don't want any?" he says.

I draw the line at cannibalism. "No thanks, I aint hungry."

I change the subject. "Zach ever say what he want to do when he grow up?"

"Not lately. When he was little, he say he wanna be a astronaut, but he aint said nothin' like that in a long time now."

AN ASTRONAUT IS A HUMAN TRAINED IN ENGINEERING AND THE SKILL OF FLYING AIRPLANES. HE GOES INTO SPACE BEYOND THE SKY. THEY ARE HIGHLY ADMIRED BY HUMANS.

Sounds like they have to have a lot of education.

YES, THEY NEED AT LEAST ONE COLLEGE DEGREE.

Maybe this is a way to convince Zach he needs to be more serious about school and stay away from the Darrells of this world?

I clean up lunch while Moline goes into his room to change clothes. I hear the water running in the bathroom, and I assume he's using the thing they call a 'shower'. He emerges a half hour later looking fresh and smelling like lilacs.

"Mmm, you smell good," I say.

"Thanks. Why don't you take a shower and put on some the clothes I bought ya?"

"Okay, I'll do that 'fore Zach gets home."

I pick out an outfit and go to the bathroom to shower. I see how to open the door to the little room and walk inside.

TAKE OFF YOUR CLOTHES FIRST.

I walk out of the shower and strip naked. I catch a glimpse of myself in the mirror over the sink and admire my new body for a moment. It does have a certain beauty, but there's almost no fur at all. I shiver a bit in the air-conditioned atmosphere before I return to the shower.

NOW, THE KNOB ON THE LEFT IS FOR HOT WATER AND THE ONE ON THE RIGHT IS FOR COLD WATER. TURN BOTH KNOBS UNTIL THE WATER RUNS OUT THAT SPOUT AT THE RIGHT TEMPERATURE.

I do as the Great Spirit commands and finally get it just right.

NOW, PUSH IN THAT LITTLE PLUNGER AND THE WATER WILL COME OUT OF THE SHOWER HEAD ABOVE YOU.

I jump back as cold water hits my skin, but it quickly turns warm, and I revel in the soothing warmth and the feel of the little jets on my skin.

USE THE SOAP IN THAT TRAY TO CLEAN YOUR SKIN.

I find the soap and notice that's where Moline's aroma comes from. I rub it on my skin and rinse it off then step from the shower.

USE THAT CLOTH ON THE RACK TO DRY YOURSELF. HUMANS CALL IT A TOWEL.

I take one of the towels and rub it on my skin, marveling at the sensation. I resolve to do a shower as often as possible. I dress in new clothes and rejoin Moline in the kitchen. He beames when he sees me.

"You look like a real lady now, and you sure smell a lot better."

"Thanks. I feel better. Thanks again for the new clothes. I'll try ta pay ya someday."

"Cookin' an' cleanin'll be pay 'nough. We've needed a woman's hand 'round here for a long time."

A sad overcast dulls his usually cheerful face.

"You must miss her a lot," I say.

"Sure do, she could prob'ly help with Zach. But she done gone."

"I watched my brothers go through teenage. I talked ta him some when he come home last night, but I need ta talk with him some more."

"I wish you would. He don't pay me much 'tention."

At that point Zach comes in.

"Hey Daddy, hey Jaqueen," he says. The greeting is

perfunctory, but he does a double take on me. "You get some new clothes?"

I stand and model for him. "Thanks to yo Daddy."

"Looks good," he says as he heads for his room.

In a few minutes Zach returns in a sweatshirt, shorts and athletic shoes. He heads for the door. "See y'all later."

Moline's stern voice stops him. "Where you goin'? How 'bout homework?"

"Got a game at the schoolyard. Today's Friday, don't got ta do no homework 'til Sunday."

I add my admonition, "You be back fo supper, heah?"

"I be back in time fo your cookin', Jaqueen. Bye."

"What is fo supper? Better cook the rest o' them rabbits 'fore they get too old."

THERE IS HAM IN THE REFRIGERATOR. TELL HIM YOU'LL COOK THAT.

"Wouldn't you like some ham fo a change? You had rabbit fo lunch."

"Sounds good to me. I think I'll do some fishin' 'fore supper."

He gathers some equipment from a cabinet and walks out the door.

He isn't gone long when Zach comes in with a worried expression.

"What happen to yo game?" I ask.

"Didn't play, not enough guys." He starts for his room.

HE'S LYING, CALL HIM BACK.

"Wait a minute. Somethin's wrong. Sit y'all down and tell me 'bout it."

He stands in thought for a moment then takes a seat at the kitchen table.

"Promise you won't tell Daddy?"

"This is just 'tween you an' me." I sit down opposite him.

"Darrell want me ta sell, an' I say no. He laugh and so do the other bros. He say I can make money like he does if I want."

"You mean sellin' dope?"

"Yeah, but …"

I cut him off, "You know that a crime, don't ya?"

He looks at the table-top and begins to trace out a pattern around the wood grain. "Yeah, but what can I do?"

"You can say no jus' like you did. You wanna wind up in jail?"

He snorts in disgust. "I aint gonna go to jail. I'm a juvenile. I'd go to detention."

"All the same thing, aint it? You still aint free."

He turns his head away from me and looks out the window as if expecting someone or something to come to his rescue but says nothing.

"Look, Darrell aint your friend. He just lookin' for another pusher so he can make more money. You tell me if this aint how it go down. He give you th' stuff, and it's up ta you ta sell it to some poor kid who don't know no different. He takes a big cut off what you make, but it's never 'nough. He got all kinds o' reasons why he need more o' what you gets. You get behind an' soon he's on your case cause you owe him money. If you don't want no beatin', you gotta find more poor suckers t' buy your stuff. But Darrell's already got most o' th' kids hooked that gonna be hooked. You gotta start sellin' t' tramps an' bums. Soon, they behind on payin' you, but they needs a fix. Now, you got Darrell after you 'sides them bums an' the kids that aint got money anymore. You start packin' heat an' robbin' the 7/11 to pay Darrell. Then, you gits caught for either dope or robbery, or shootin' somebody an' you in jail. You not only ruin th' lives o' all those kids, you done ruined your own."

He hangs his head and runs his hands along his thighs. "What can I do, Jaqueen?"

"First thing, you can stop hangin' 'round with Darrell and his gang."

He shakes his head with a sad expression. "They's th' only cool gang at school. Aint nobody else."

"Theys gotta be somebody at that school what wants ta make somethin' respectable outta themselves."

He snorts again. "Yeah, nerds. I aint no nerd."

I sit back in my chair and shake my head. "You think doctors are nerds? How 'bout lawyers, engineers, businessmen? How 'bout astronauts?"

The last one makes him sit up and come alert.

"Astronauts aint no nerds."

"You could be a astronaut."

He laughs and waves a dismissive hand at me. "They all got college degrees. I'll never get no degree."

"Why not?"

"You gotta have money for college, and we aint got no money."

"They's scholarships, and you could get a summer job an' save up. I know your Daddy'd help all he could."

My suggestion provokes mild laughter. "Summer job, huh? What I make, $10 a hour? I sell dope for Darrell I make that much in five minutes. If I wants college, I can save more money from sellin' dope."

"You like basketball. You any good?"

He smiles at this question and sits more upright. "Yeah, I th' best shooter they is."

"If you that good, why you not on th' school team?"

"That aint cool."

"Cool or not, some college might want you ta play fo them. They'd give y'all a free education just fo playin' ball."

"I tol' ya, that aint cool. Can I go now?"

I see this is going to get me nowhere. I'm failing my first assignment. What can I do, Great Spirit?I

YOU'VE DONE ALL YOU CAN RIGHT NOW. YOU'VE WARNED HIM. NOW, HE MUST SEE THE WISDOM IN YOUR WORDS. HE MUST 'HIT BOTTOM', AND THAT MAY BE VERY PAINFUL FOR EVERYONE INVOLVED, BUT IT HAS TO HAPPEN.

"Okay, all I can do is tell you what I know. You gotta make up your own mind what kind o' life y'all wants."

"I knows what I's doin', Jaqueen." With that, he leaves the table and goes to his room, I hope to study.

I'm getting ready to cook dinner when Moline comes in with five fish on a line. "Fishin' was good. Look here." He holds them up for me. I remember when I was an eagle and ate that kind of fish. They were good.

"I'll clean 'em up for supper," he says and takes them outside after replacing his fishing gear in the cabinet.

How do I cook fish?

DON'T WORRY. I'LL WALK YOU THROUGH IT. IT'S JUST LIKE THE CHICKEN. ROAST SOME POTATOES AND OPEN A CAN OF HOMINY WHILE YOU'RE WAITING FOR HIM TO CLEAN THE FISH.

I do as the Great Spirit says, and Moline soon comes in with the fish. The heads and insides are gone, but they still have skin. As far as an eagle's concerned, he's thrown away the best parts.

"You know how t' fillet 'em, or do I hafta do that?" he says.

TELL HIM YOU DO.

"Course I do. You go get cleaned up fo supper." I shoo him out of the kitchen as I take the platter of fish from him.

What now?

The Great Spirit walks me through filleting the fish and frying them in a style he claims Moline likes. He also teaches me how to make something called 'hush puppies'.

Zach joins us for supper.

"This is the best fish I ever tasted," Zach says as he reloads his plate.

"And no bones at all," Moline says. "You did a good job filleting them fish."

I just smile at both of them and secretly give thanks to the Great Spirit. "Thank y'all, but I was taught by a expert."

After supper, Zach and Moline watch TV while I clean up. Television is interesting. The pictures are so real, and they seem to be enthralled by it. When I'm finished, I excuse myself and walk outside for a while. I like to listen to the sounds of the bayou. The frogs are calling for mates, and the gators are groaning their displeasure with nearly everything.

Maybe I should be a gator tonight? I laugh. It's still gator season, and I wouldn't want to be hunted. I decide to sleep inside and rejoin Zach and Moline just as they are turning off the TV and heading for bed.

Chapter 3

Saturday, Zach's dresses for basketball when he comes out for breakfast. Moline and I are just finishing. Zach grabs a biscuit and heads for the door.

"Sit down an' have some breakfast," Moline commands.

Zach protests, "I'll be late."

Moline freezes his son with a look of pure authority. "Y'all'll play better basketball if you have some food in you. Now sit down."

Zach slips into a chair as I hand him a plate of pancakes and a glass of orange juice. He gobbles it all down in record time and rises. "Can I go now?"

"Just be back for supper," Moline admonishes.

After Zach is gone, I sit down with Moline. "You know who he's runnin' with don't you?"

"I know, but they aint much I can do 'bout it. I've talked my head off to that boy. Nothin' seems to sink into that thick skull o' his."

"I know. I tried to talk to him too, but it didn't do no good. I know what you mean," I say.

"Let's go get us some gators," he says.

Somehow, I have a feeling Zach is going to need me. I beg off.

"I got lots o' housework to do and laundry 'sides. I better stay home today."

"Okay, I could use the help, but I'll get by." He folds his napkin on the table and leaves the cabin.

I clear the table and do the dishes before the Great Spirit helps me with understanding the machinery humans use to clean their clothes. Why they have to have clothes is a mystery to me. Why can't they just go around in their natural state like us animals? Maybe it's because they've lost almost all their fur? Anyway, I dust and vacuum while the clothes are washing and drying.

Once the clothes are back in their storage bins, I transform into a hawk and go in search of Zach.

I fly in ever increasing circles until I spot him at a park with a group of other boys. They aren't playing basketball. Three boys are lounging near one of the mechanical devices humans use to get from place to place. They call them cars.

One of the boys seems to be in charge, and I guess he must be Darrell. I don't know what Zach sees in him. He's not tall or well built, and he's not even good looking. His skin is two shades darker than Zach's and his features are heavy. He wears his hair in a flat-top that rises two inches above his scalp. He's dressed in jeans and a hoodie and wears athletic shoes. The two other boys in the group are dressed in a like manner.

I spot a tree nearby and land on a branch where I can hear their conversation. Zach finishes his basketball game and greets the gang.

"Hey, Darrell, hey guys. Whose car is that?"

"It's my uncle's car. He's letting me have it for the afternoon," Darrell says.

HE'S LYING. IT IS HIS UNCLE'S CAR, BUT HE STOLE THE KEYS WHILE HIS UNCLE WAS SPACED OUT ON DRUGS.

"What we gonna do today?" Zach says.

"We gonna go cruisin' and find some babes," one of the other boys says. "You commin' 'long?"

"Sure, let's go," Zach agrees all too readily.

The boys pile into the car and I follow them up a highway to Franklin where they stop at a convenience store.

DARRELL'S UNCLE IS AWAKE NOW AND HAS REPORTED HIS CAR STOLEN.

I circle the parking lot where the car is parked and listen to the boys as they harass each girl who enters the store. Thank goodness Zach is hanging in the background. It gives me hope he can be salvaged.

THE MANAGER OF THE CONVENIENCE STORE HAS CALLED THE POLICE ABOUT THE BOYS.

I broaden my circles and spot a car marked "police" heading for the store. I wish there were some way I could warn Zach, but I can't change back to human form now. He'd never understand how I got here. I swoop low over his head.

"Hey, look out. That bird almost got ya," Darrell shouts.

"You got a mouse in yo hair?" the boy they call Leeroy asks.

Zach rubs his head automatically then blushes at his reaction to the question. "Aw Leeroy," he says.

I buzz Zach again. This time Darrell pulls a pistol from under his hoodie.

"I'll take care o' that bird," he says and points it at me. I know pistols, so I dive for the cover of the trees nearby. Zach doesn't seem to get the hint anyway. I watch hidden in the branches as the police car pulls into the parking lot. One policeman approaches the boys while another stands outside the car shielded by the car door.

Darrell quickly puts his gun away, but the policeman has

spotted it.

"I need to see your permit for that pistol," the officer says.

"My Daddy say I don't need no permit," Darrell counters.

"But the state of Louisiana says you do. You got one?"

Darrell shakes his head no.

"I'll take the gun please. Your father can come and get it at the Franklin police headquarters." He holds out a hand toward Darrell.

Darrell looks at the hand with contempt and then stares at the policeman's face.

"Give it to him, Darrell," the boy they've called Achmed says. "We don't want no trouble with the law."

"You come and take it," Darrell says to the officer as he lifts his hoodie to reveal the pistol tucked in his pants.

The officer takes the gun, and I notice the officer at the car use what the humans call a radio. As the first officer inspects the pistol for safety purposes the other officer calls to him, "We've got a want on the car." He draws his gun and trains it on Darrell. The first officer tucks Darrell's gun in his waistband and draws his own. "Is this your car?" he asks.

"It's my uncle's car. I just borrowed it for a while," Darrell responds.

"That's not what he says. You boys are under arrest. We'll go down to the station and you can sort this out with your uncle. Call for back-up Charlie."

"Already have. They're on their way," Charlie responds.

Another police car pulls into the lot. By now, a small crowd has gathered, and a rather large black man approaches the officer.

"No need for guns, officer. What've these boys done?"

The officer holsters his pistol, but the one at the car continues to hold his at the ready.

"First, the manager of this store complained these boys were creating a disturbance outside his store. Second, this boy was carrying a handgun without a permit, and he's obviously under 21. Third, the car he's driving has been reported as stolen. Now please let us get on with our work, sir."

"I just want you to know I'm a lawyer, and I'll be watching this situation carefully."

"I understand, now please step back."

The lawyer turns to Darrell. "You want me to help you, son?"

Darrell looks at him with the most innocent look you could imagine. "We was just havin' some fun with some girls we know, an' I'm sorry 'bout th' gun, but my Daddy say I don't need no permit in Louisiana. An' 'bout this car, my uncle always lets me have it when I need it. I got a driver's license an' I left him a note 'bout me takin' it. I'd 'preciate it if'n y'all'd help us out, sir."

I haven't been around humans that long, but I can tell his story is a pack of lies, even from up here is this tree.

"I'm Wilson Guidry," he hands the officer a card, "and I'm now representing these boys. I'll see you at the station house."

Two more police cars arrive, and two of those officers step out and join the one with the boys.

"Watcha got, Bob?" one asks.

"We need to take these kids in for questioning, and we need a tow truck for this stolen car."

"Allegedly stolen, officer," Guidry says.

If he knew what I know, he wouldn't use that word.

The boys are herded into two police cars while one car waits for the tow truck. I follow the police cars to a building marked as a police station. I land on the roof and change into a mosquito in order to get inside. I fly down and land on Zach's hoodie. I resist the urge to bite him even though I feel rather hungry.

The boys are lined up on a bench in a hallway with an officer standing guard over them. A policeman, the lawyer and Darrell enter a room across the hallway, but I stay with Zach, fighting off the urge to bite someone else.

DARRELL IS TELLING THE SAME STORY INSIDE THAT ROOM HE TOLD THE OFFICER BEFORE. THE COP CAN'T MAKE HIM CHANGE IT. THE LAWYER'S ENDED THE SESSION.

The group emerges, and the policeman calls for one of the other boys. Another officer takes Darrell down the hallway. Leeroy enters the room.

THIS ONE SAYS HE WAS JUST ALONG FOR THE RIDE. THEY'RE RELEASING HIM.

Leeroy is also escorted down the hallway, and the one called Achmed goes in leaving Zach alone. My mosquito sense tells me his blood pressure is high and he's sweating even though the hallway is cool. He's scared.

SAME STORY FROM THIS ONE.

At last Zach is called in. The lawyer indicates he should sit next to him, and Zach takes the chair.
"What's your name, son?" the policeman asks.
"Zach, Zach Thibodeaux."
"Where do you live, Zach?"
"My Daddy's got a place on Grand Lake near Charenton."
"What were you doing with Darrell today?"

"Darrell wanted ta go cruisin', an' I said I'd go along."

"Did he tell you about the car?"

"Yeah, he say his uncle let him have it."

"Did you have any reason to suspect the car was stolen?" the lawyer asked.

"No, sir. Darrell say his uncle let him have it, and I believe him."

I study the police officer's face and see he probably believes Zach. The lawyer turns to the policeman.

"I don't see any reason to hold this boy either. He didn't assist in the car theft, and he was not armed."

The policeman rises, "Okay, you can go call your father to pick you up. You're dismissed."

Zach rises, and the lawyer accompanies him to a holding room where the other boys are waiting.

"You okay?" Darrell asks.

"Yeah, I'm good. How 'bout you?"

"They called my uncle. When he find out it was me with the car, he told 'em he found my note, an' it was okay. He's gonna come get me. Y'all can ride home with us if you wants to."

The lawyer contradicts Darrell, "No you can't. Each of you boys will have to be picked up by someone in your family. The police can't let you go with anyone else."

Zach says, "I guess I gotta call Daddy. Where's a phone?"

The policeman in the room points to a wall phone. "You can call from over there. Dial 9 first to get an outside line."

The boy named Leeroy approaches Zach. "You got a skeeter on your shoulder. I'll git it." He raises a hand to strike, and I avoid the blow easily. I hide in the lawyer's afro figuring he'll be leaving the station soon. I have to hurry back to the cabin to be there when Zach calls.

Once outside, I change into a hawk again and fly back to the cabin. Moline isn't back from hunting gators yet, and the phone's ringing as I walk in.

"Hello," I answer playing dumb about all that's happened.

"Hi Jaqueen, this is Zach. Is my Daddy home yet?"

"No, he aint back yet. Where you at?"

His voice takes on a sheepish tone. "I'm at the police station in Franklin."

"What you doin' there?"

"I was cruisin' with Darrell, and the cops thought he'd stolen his uncle's car so they 'rested us. It's okay though. It was all a mistake and we're free to go, but Daddys got ta come get me."

"I don't know when he'll be home, but I'll tell him as soon as he gets here. He's gonna be mad as hell y'know."

"I know. I'll explain it all to him when he gets here."

"Okay, he be back soon."

I hang up and think about what to say to Zach later.

A few minutes later, I hear Moline's airboat approaching. It stops at the dock, and Moline comes in disheveled and sweat soaked from gator hunting. The smell of the bayou radiates from his swamp-soaked clothes.

"Hey, Jaqueen," he greets me.

"Sit down, I got sometin' to tell y'all."

He takes a chair at the kitchen table and looks at me with a troubled expression. "What's up?"

"You gotta go get Zach at the Franklin police station."

"Is he in trouble?" He rises partially, and I gently push him back into the seat.

"No, not this time. He went cruisin' with Darrell and some of

Darrell's friends. The problem was, Darrell took his uncle's car without askin'. The uncle reported it stolen, and the cops picked 'em up. When the uncle found out Darrell had the car, he called off the theft charge, but the police'll only release the boys to a parent."

Moline relaxes visibly now that he knows Zach was just a passenger. "I guess I'd better clean up and go get him."

"I'll get supper ready while you're gone. Don't be too hard on th' boy, now."

"He won't get anything he don't deserve." With that, he leaves for the shower.

A while later, he emerges looking very fatherly. "See you later."

I hear the thing he calls a pickup come to life, and I decide to hear what he says to Zach. I step outside and transform into a mosquito again. I barely make it to the inside of the pickup before he pulls away.

During the ride into Franklin, I observe his operation of the pickup. The coordination of his hands, feet and eyes is remarkable.

YOU COULD LEARN TO DO THAT IN A FEW DAYS.

Oh, Great Spirit, I'd love to be able to do what he's doing. Would he teach me?

I'M SURE HE WOULD, BUT YOU'D HAVE TO GET A DRIVER'S LICENSE, AND WE DON'T HAVE TIME FOR THAT. BESIDES, YOU CAN MAKE BETTER TIME AS A HAWK.

I might have to use the pickup some time as a human, and I'd like to know how.

MAYBE ON YOUR NEXT ASSIGNMENT.

What he says makes sense, but I decided to ask Moline to teach me after I get Zach on the right track.

At the station, I ride in on Moline's shoulder. The desk sergeant calls up Zach who has a hard time looking his father in the eye.

"Hi Daddy,"

"Hi yourself, let's go home."

The air in the pickup is quite frosty, but Moline breaks the ice.

"You learn anything from this?" he asks.

"Yes Daddy."   Zach stares out the window at the passing scenery.

"What you learn?"

"Cops aint no friend o' black people."

"Don't give me that 'victim' stuff. They mistreat you?"

"No, but some black lawyer guy helped us out. He was standin' 'round when the cops came up to Darrell's car, and he stayed with us 'til everything got straightened out. I don't know what might o' happened if he wasn't there. He gave us each one o' his cards. I got it here in my billfold."

"I aint sayin' the cops can't be racist, but don't blame 'em for what Darrell did. That kid's trouble."

Zach resumes his study or the passing foliage, and I decide I need to get busy with supper. I leave the pickup through the open window and fight the buffeting slip stream until I can fly someplace to become a hawk.

Chapter 4

I'm busy with pots and pans when the pickup pulls into the drive.

Zach goes straight to his room without a word, and Moline says, "What's for supper?"

"I found some of them little bugs in the freezer. What you call 'em?"

"They's crawdads. That sounds good." He goes to the fridge and opens a beer before sitting down at the kitchen table.

Okay, Great Spirit, what do I do with these crawdads?

Great Spirit guides me through the process of fixing supper while Moline sips his beer. He finally breaks the silence.

"What we gonna do to get that boy away from that hoodlum Darrell?"

I talk while going through the actions of preparing supper. "He thinks Darrell's cool. Maybe this here brush with th' law'll make him see that boy aint cool, just trouble. I'll keep talkin' to him."

"You can try. He sure don't pay much 'tention to what I say."

After supper, I talk to Zach.

"Take a little walk with me Zach, please?"

He looks at me for a moment wanting to say no, but he finally smiles and says, "Okay, Jaqueen."

We step outside into the bayou twilight and I signal we should sit on a log near the water.

"You know Darrell should be in jail, don't you?" I ask.

"No way. It was all just a mistake."

"No, it wasn't no 'mistake'. Darrell didn't leave no note. His uncle just covered for him 'cause Darrell's his supplier."

"You don't know that. You guessin'."

"No, I'm not. A woman's got ways o' knowin' things. Want to know the name o' th' lawyer what helped you?"

"You don't know that. I got his card here in my billfold, and you aint seen it."

"See if his name's Wilson Guidry."

I smile as he opens his billfold and scans the card. His eyes grow as big as an owl's eyes, and his chin drops a mile.

"That's right. How you know that?"

"Like I said, a woman's got ways."

"You a voodoo Mama-Loa or somethin'?"

I place a hand on his shoulder. "No, Zach, but I'm blessed with a way o' knowin' things that happen, an' I know Darrell's no good. You stay with him, and you gonna be in big trouble pretty soon. You saw he had a gun, didn't ya?"

"Yeah, but he wouldn't use it t' hurt nobody. It's just for protection."

"Don't believe that. If he got a gun, he gonna hurt somebody sometime."

He hangs his head and studies the water in the lake for a moment. "If I don't hang out with Darrell, who I hang out with?"

It's a fair question. I turn to the Great Spirit for an answer.

THERE'S A GIRL HE LIKES AT SCHOOL. TELL HIM TO TALK TO HER.

"Aint there no girls you like at school?"

He smiles broadly. "Sure is. Myra LeBlanc's real pretty."

"Why don't you try hangin' out with her?"

He shakes his head, and his face takes on a sad expression. "She's always with two or three other girls."

"You a good-lookin' boy. If'n she thought you was interested in her she'd talk ta you 'stead o' them girls."

"That's okay, but I still need some bros to hang with, and Darrell's gang's the coolest bunch."

"What other 'bros' you got at school?"

He thinks a moment before answering, and the Great Spirit breaks in.

THE MATH CLUB HAS TWO BOYS HE KNOWS AS MEMBERS. HE'S GOOD AT MATH. HE COULD JOIN THEM. BESIDES, THE LEBLANC GIRL GOES TO SOME OF THEIR MEETINGS

"What about the Math Club?" I ask.

"I thought 'bout that. I like Math."

"Give it a try. Anything but Darrell."

He smiles at me and shakes his head. "I still don't know how you know 'bout Darrell and his uncle."

"You convinced I'm right?'

"Yeah, but I gots to know how you know."

"Y'all never mind that for now. Maybe I'll tell you later on. Just don't tell yo Daddy I got the power, okay?"

"Okay, but you gotta tell me sometime."

"I will, but it's gotta be our secret for now."

"Okay, Jaqueen."

By now, the bayou has grown dark, and the chorus of the night animals almost drowns out conversation. "Let's go back inside," I say, and we return to the cabin and Moline.

He turns from the TV to Zach. "Jaqueen, talk any sense into

you, boy?" he says.

"Maybe, but don't ever doubt anything she say," Zach responds as he goes toward his room.

Moline shouts after him, "Remember we got church tomorrow."

"I got it, Daddy," Zach shouts back.

Moline turns to me. "What's he talkin' 'bout?"

"Oh, nothin' just a joke 'tween us two," I say.

Moline grunts his understanding and changes the subject. "You Catholic or Protestant?"

I have no idea about religion, so I turn to the Great Spirit.

MOLINE'S BAPTIST. THEY'RE A BIT ON THE FUNDAMENTALIST SIDE, BUT GOOD PEOPLE. TELL HIM YOU'RE BAPTIST.

"I'm Baptist," I say.

"Good, you can go to church with us it y'all want?"

CHURCH COULD BE A GOOD INFLUENCE ON ZACH. I'M HAVING THE LeBLANC FAMILY START GOING TO MOLINE'S CHURCH. MAYBE ZACH'LL BE MORE INTERESTED IN CHURCH IF HE KNOWS SHE'S THERE.

"I'd like that."

Moline thinks a moment. "You aint got no fancy dress for church, but I gots a couple o' things my late wife wore. I kept 'em 'cause she looked so good in 'em. She was a bit bigger'n you, though. I'll bring 'em out an' you can try 'em on."

He goes into his room and returns carrying two dresses. "You can see if these fits y'all."

I pick the bright orange one and take it to the bathroom. It is a bit large and hangs on me like a shroud.

I CAN TAKE CARE OF THIS.

A flash of light, and the dress suddenly fits like a glove. I admire myself in the door mirror. Clothes do make the woman. I go back to model for Moline.

He whistles softly. "I never thought you and Wanda could be th' same size, but you sure look good in that." His gaze shifts to my feet. "Those Nikes don't go with that dress. Your feet is so big I know her shoes won't come close to fittin' y'all."

I remember the Great Spirits magic. "Let me try a pair."

Once more he goes into his room and brings out a pair of shoes matching the dress. I take them to the bathroom where the Great Spirit once more makes them fit. They're high heels, and I'm a bit wobbly going back to Moline.

He shakes his head in disbelief. "No way. She had such tiny feet, and yours is number nines for sure."

"They don't hurt none," I say. I figure big feet are a carry-over from my rabbit form.

"I don't know how you did it, but you'll be the hit of Grand Lake First Baptist Church in th' mornin'." He consults his watch. "Better get to bed now. I'll wake you up at six when I get up. Good night Jaqueen."

"Nite, Moline."

Chapter 5

Sunday morning, I shower and dress. The Great Spirit helps me do my hair. The men are very impressed with my looks.

"Umm umm, you look like a movie star even if you do have big feet and long ears," Moline says.

"You sure foxy, Jaqueen," Zach adds.

"Thank you, gents," I say as we board the pickup and head for what they call 'church'.

I don't quite know what to expect at 'church'. I know it's a place humans go to worship the Great Spirit, so it must be a nice place. As we walk in, people greet Moline and Zach. Moline introduces me as his cousin who's staying with them for a while.

The women are dressed even more finely than I am, and most of them are wearing extravagant hats. We take a seat as the service begins with a joyous song. I don't know the tune or the words, but the Great Spirit coaches me along. I glance at Zach and see his eyes are fixed on a young girl two pews ahead of us. We sit when the song is finished, and I whisper to Zach.

"You lookin' at someone?"

He leans closer to me and whispers a reply, "That's Myra LeBlanc from my school. I didn't know she came here."

I nod my head knowingly and return my attention to the minister. When the service is over, Zach says to his father, "Daddy, I gotta talk to somebody for a minute, okay?"

Moline nods approval, and Zach heads straight for Myra and her parents.

I can tell by the smile on the girl's face she's happy to see Zach.

I THINK WE HAVE A BUDDING ROMANCE THERE.

Let's hope so.

All the way back home Zach can only talk about Myra. Moline smiles all the way, and I cross my fingers, hoping this may be the start of separating Zach from Darrell.

*****

Zach's off to school Monday, and Moline has used all his gator tags, so, he tells me he's going back to work at the Sterling Sugar plant in Franklin. I'm glad he'll be gone most of the day so I can keep an eye on Zach after school.

As soon as Moline is off to work, I turn into a hawk and fly to Zach's school. I circle the schoolyard, but there are no students there. I do spot several chipmunks though, and I decide to have lunch.

After two chipmunks, I nap in a tree until school's out. I perch where I can observe the kids and spot Zach exiting with Myra. Darrell and his crowd are lounging near his uncle's car in the school parking lot. I take off and circle above them. They spot Zach and Myra and begin to heckle Zach.

"Hey, Zach's in love," Leeroy shouts.

"She got a nice ass," Achmed chimes in.

Zach excuses himself from Myra and confronts the gang with clenched fists.

"Hey, Myra's a nice girl. I don't want y'all sayin' that stuff 'round her," he says.

"Take it easy, man. We's just funning ya," Darrell says.

Zach relaxes a bit but keeps a stern expression. "Well, okay, but the next guy what makes a crack at her gonna get a knuckle sandwich."

"Okay, okay, we'll cool it with her," Darrell says. "Come on with us. We gonna get even with that cracker store manager what called the cops on us."

Zach steps back a bit and looks at him with a skeptical eye. "What you gonna do?"

"Nothin' much. We just gonna relieve him o' some o' his inventory, that's all."

"I aint in for no shopliftin'," Zach protests.

Leeroy breaks in. "If you don't help us out this time, we aint never gonna let you hang with us again."

"Yeah, come on, Zach. We needs y'all." Achmed says.

Darrell puts an arm around Zach's shoulders. "Look, all you gots t' do is lift a candy bar, or somethin' small like that. You walk outta th' store, and nobody knows you got it. We'll take care o' the big stuff, okay?"

"Well, long as nobody gets hurt," Zach says.

"Nah, no rough stuff, just fun," Darrell assures him.

They pile into the car and head for the convenience store while I follow from above. When they reach the store, I transform into a mosquito and park on the ceiling of the store. The boys begin their shoplifting spree. Zach grabs a candy bar and stuffs it into his pocket while the other boys attack larger items. Darrell is the bravest. He attempts to hide a six pack of beer, but the manager spots him.

"Hey, you, put that six pack back," he yells.

Darrell gives him a one finger salute and starts to walk out of the store. The manager flies over the counter to intercept him while he shouts, "Call the cops," to the cashier.

Darrell pulls the pistol from under his hoodie, and fires. I quickly dive to Zach's leg and bite him as painfully as possible.

He bends over and slaps at his leg in reaction to the attack. He barely misses squashing me, but he's below the shelving which absorbs the shotgun blast from the cashier's weapon.

Other shots follow from Darrell's pistol, but Zach stays down.

"Come on, Zach. Let's git outta here," Darrell shouts as he runs to the door.

Zach peers cautiously around the shelves. The store manager is sitting on the floor bleeding from a wound in his right arm while the cashier is busy reloading her shotgun. The sound of tires squealing calls his attention to Darrell and the other boys making their getaway without him. Two police cars arrive, and one takes off after Darrell's car while the other pulls up to the front of the store. I'm proud of Zach when he returns the stolen candy bar to the shelf.

He steps from behind the shelves with his hands held high.

"Don't shoot. I aint part o' that bunch."

The cashier lowers her shotgun as two policemen enter the store with drawn weapons.

"This guy's hurt, Jeff. Call for an ambulance," one of the policemen orders. He turns to the manager, "What happened?"

"Some kids were in here shoplifting. When I challenged 'em, one kid pulled a gun and started shooting. Beth fired at them but didn't hit anybody. They took off just before you got here."

The other officer comes into the store. "Ambulance is on the way."

"Okay, I don't think he's hurt too badly. Looks like the bleeding's about stopped."

The manager points to Zach. "He was with 'em."

The officer rises and comes to Zach. "That true?"

"Yes, sir. I came in with 'em, but I didn't know there was

goin' ta be any shootin'."

"I'm gonna search you now. Put your hands above your head."

Zach complies, and the officer pats him down.

"Nothin' here, but you had plenty o' time to put everything back. Tell me about your buddies."

"We go to Franklin High School. They was just gonna come here for some stuff, but Darrell, he's the boss o' th' gang, started stealin' stuff. When that guy yelled at him, Darrell pulled his gun. I got bit by a skeeter and ducked just as everybody started shootin'. I didn't see nothin'."

"You stick around. You'll need to make a statement at police headquarters, but I don't think you'll be charged with anything." He turns to the manager. "This kid do anything?"

"If he didn't steal anything, he's okay."

At that point, the ambulance arrives. Emergency medics begin to attend to the manager while the police officers take statements from the cashier and the one other customer in the store during the incident. An officer places Zach in the back of a police car.

I think it's time for me to get back to the cabin to be there when the police call. I leave the store, transform into a hawk and fly back.

I don't have to wait long for the phone call. I advise them his father is at work and won't be able to come for him until later.

That evening I have to give Moline another dose of bad news about his son. He reacts with anger.

"This is the last time I go after that boy. He can rot in that jail if it happens again," he says.

"Don't be angry with him. He really innocent this time."

He looks at me with a quizzical expression. "How do you know?"

"Like I told Zach, women have ways of knowing."

He rubs his chin and stares at me. "He told me I should believe anything you say, but I don't know 'bout this."

"Believe me, he is innocent. Just go get him, and don't be mad at him. This may be the way we get him away from Darrell and his gang."

"Okay, but we need to talk to him before we have dinner."

Moline leaves, and I prepare a dinner that can wait, thanks to help from the Great Spirit.

I hear the pickup pull in and await their entrance.

A stern-faced Moline marches a contrite Zach to the kitchen table, and I join them.

"What happened?" I ask, pretending I wasn't there.

"It was bad this time, Jaqueen. Darrell shot a guy."

I pretend horror. "My God! Did he kill him?"

"No, but the cops got him and the other guys, and they're in big trouble."

"What were you doing there?" Moline asks.

Zach hangs his head even lower than I thought possible. "They was gonna do some shopliftin' there to get even with that store manager what called the cops on us th' last time, an' I agreed to help 'em, but I didn't do no shopliftin'. I only had to tell the police what happened, and they let me go."

"He'll have to testify at their trial," Moline adds.

I move to Zach and put my arms around him. "You poor boy. I'm glad you stayed out of that trouble, but now you know what hangin' 'round with that bunch can get you into."

Zach pats my arm and smiles at me. "I sure do. I aint gonna

hang with those guys no more."

"I'm glad you learned your lesson, son. Now let's have supper."

Chapter 6

The next day I take my hawk form and follow Zach to school. To my surprise, Darrell and his gang are waiting for Zach just outside the schoolyard.

"Hey rat, what you tell those cops?" Darrell shouts.

Zach walks over to them, and I don't like the looks of the other boys. I think they mean to hurt Zach.

"I told 'em what went down, that's all. No tellin' what kind o' story that manager might've made up to make things worse. How'd you guys get outa jail?"

"I called that lawyer guy what helped us last time, an' he got us out on bail. He said you'd have t' testify at our trial," Darrell answers.

"That's right. I'll tell the same story there I told the cops."

The boys crowd around Zach with menacing faces and clenched fists. I don't like the way things are going, and I transform into a large wolf. I stay well back but remain ready to pounce on the first boy to threaten Zach.

"We want you ta say that gal shot first, or we don't want you to testify at all, understand?" Darrell says,

Zach assumes a belligerent attitude. "My Daddy say I gotta tell the truth if'n they calls me."

Darrell's mouth takes on a twisted grin. "You can't testify if'n you's sick, now can y'all?"

The boys edge closer, and Darrell takes a knife from his pocket and opens the blade. Zach takes a step back. "You can't do nothin' here. Too many people t' see."

"No, but now you know we mean business. You testify that gal shot first, and we're still friends."

I'm proud of Zach. He faces up to Darrell and speaks tough words. "I aint your friend no more, Darrell, so I don't care 'bout that."

The school bell rings, and the other kids start entering the building.

"Maybe I should give you somethin' t' remind y'all we means business?" Darrell snarls.

The other two boys grab Zach, and Darrell starts toward him with the knife. That's it. I charge Darrell and catch him completely by surprise. I grip the wrist of the hand holding the knife tasting blood soaking through his sleeve. He drops the knife with a howl of pain and falls to the sidewalk. Zach shakes loose from the other stunned boys and runs into the school building. I beat a hasty retreat into some woods across the street and transform into a mosquito.

"You aint heard the last o' this, Zach Thibodeaux," Darrell yells after Zach. He turns to his buddies, "Get that dog! I'm gonna kill it."

They run into the woods, but they're looking for a dog, and I'm a mosquito. I fly inside the school building and find Zach at the principal's office. I fly to the ceiling and listen.

"What can I do for you, Zach?" the principal asks.

"It's Darrell and his gang. They got into some trouble in Franklin, and I was with 'em."

The principal leans back in his swivel chair and frowns. "I've heard about their trouble. I'm glad you haven't been charged."

"But I's involved. I gotta testify at they trial, and they don't want me to tell the true story. Darrell, Leeroy and Achmed stopped me outside the school and Darrell pulled a knife on me. He said I'd better tell the story their way, or else. What should I do, Mr. Jordan?"

"First you report the incident to the police. I think they'll want to talk to those boys."

Mr. Jordan flips the intercom switch on his phone. "Martha, ask officer Trahan to come in, please."

A female voice responds, "Yes, sir."

"Do you ride the bus to school?"

"Yes, sir."

"Good, I'll make sure officer Trahan sees you safely on the bus this afternoon."

"Those guys know where I lives, sir."

"Is anyone home when you get off the bus?"

"Yes, sir."

"Good, call them before you leave school. You can use the school office phone."

"What 'bout that trial, sir?"

"You know you have to tell the truth in court, don't you?"

Zach hangs his head for a moment before answering. "Yes, sir."

"Then, you can't let them intimidate you."

Officer Trahan knocks, and Mr. Jordan calls, "Come in."

A burly, black police officer enters. "You wanted me, Mr. Jordan."

"Yes, do you know Zach Thebodeaux?"

The officer offers his hand, and Zach stands to take it. "Pleased to meet y'all Zach. I've seen you hangin' 'round with Darrell Hebert and his gang, haven't I?"

"Yes, sir, but that's th' problem," Zach answers.

"Zach, here, will have to testify at those boy's trial, and they stopped him and threatened him before school." Mr. Jordan explains.

"What happened?" Trahan asks.

"Darrell, Leeroy and Achmed stopped me. Leeroy and Achmed held me, and Darrell pulled out a knife and said he'd hurt me if I didn't tell the story they wanted me to tell. I think he was gonna cut me, but a big dog attacked him, and I got away."

Officer Trahan looks at Zach with a skeptical expression. "I aint seen no big dogs 'round here lately. What kind o' dog was it?"

"I don't know. It was mostly brownish with some white an' it was sure big

"Anybody else see this dog?" Trahan asks.

"I don't know. The bell rang, and ever'body went into th' school. Maybe was some other kids seen it. I don't know," Zach answers.

Trahan turns to Mr. Jordan. "Without witnesses, we'd have a hard time chargin' those boys with assault, sir."

"I'll make an announcement today for anyone who saw something to come forward. In the meantime, I want you to see that Zach gets on the buss safely after school. If you see Darrell and any of his gang on school property, you need to arrest them for truancy. I'm sure they didn't show up for classes today, but I'll let you know if they do."

"Okay, I'll be on th' lookout. See you later, Zach." Officer Trahan leaves the office, and Mr. Jordan speaks to Zach, "You can go to your classes now, Zach. Ms. Rogers will give you a hall pass."

"Yes, sir." Zach rises and leaves the office, and I follow him until he's safely in his first class.

Chapter 7

I leave the building and transform into a hawk. I circle until I spot Darrell and his pals outside a drug store. Leeroy is pouring something over my bite that makes Darrell scream in pain.

"That hurts! What is that stuff?" Darrell asks.

"Hydrogen peroxide, it kills germs, an' those dogs has lots o' germs in they'z mouths."

Leeroy puts down the bottle and begins bandaging Darrell's wrist.

"You autta get a tetanus shot," Achmed says.

"I aint gettin' no shot. I hates shots, but I'm gonna make sure that rat Zach tells the right story. That cop Trahan'll keep an eye on him when he gets on th' bus. We gotta get him when he gets off th' bus. There's a good stretch o' swamp 'tween the bus stop an' his cabin. We can take him there with no one t' see."

"I thought 'bout it some more, an' I don't want no part o' cuttin' on him," Achmed says as he shivers in reaction to the thought.

"Nah, we just gonna rough him up a bit," Darrell says.

Now that I know their plans, I can be ready for them. I fly back to the cabin and wait for Zach's call and the school bus.

At the right time, I transform into a hawk and circle above the trees. I spot Darrell, Leeroy and Achmed walking down our lane from the highway. They conceal themselves halfway to the cabin and wait for Zach. I drop to the ground between them and the bus stop and think about the best form to assume to help Zach.

I HAVE A SHAPE FOR YOU THESE BOYS HAVE NEVER SEEN.

What's that?

IT'S AN ANIMAL NOT NATIVE TO THIS REGION. IT'S A BLACK PANTHER.

I don't know what kind of an animal you're talking about.

TRUST ME, IT WILL SCARE THE WITS OUT OF THEM.

I hear the bus stop at the road. Zach is the only one who gets off here, and I soon spot him. He's wary, but I know he'll be no match for the three thugs.

Okay, Great Spirit, do your thing.

I feel a surge of strength I've never felt before with any transformation. I look down at a shiny black coat of fur on my legs. I feel as if my muscles are tightly coiled springs. I extend wicked-looking claws from my front paws and feel powerful jaws clench around long fangs. Zach is near now, and the thugs jump from their hiding place, but I spring out between them and loose a thundering snarl.

"Jesus Christ!" Darrell shouts as he jumps back at least four feet. The other two cower in place. Zach is just as frightened as they are, but he stands his ground.

"You guys lookin' for me?" Zach says, his voice a bit on the shaky side.

"What are you? Some kind o' witch or somethin'?" Leeroy asks with a voice quivering mightily.

"Yeah, you got some kind o' animal spell?" Achmed asks.

Zach is sweating profusely, but he manages a smile. "Maybe you guys shouldn't make Mother Nature angry. You know us guys what lives here in the bayou are al'ays close ta nature."

Darrell speaks, "You just call off that monster o' yours, an' we're outta here, okay?"

"I got no control over that big cat, but if he aint clawed y'all to ribbons by now, he pro'bly gonna let you go, long as you don't do nothin' ta me."

I back up next to Zach and continue to snarl at Darrell. The boys edge around me as I swipe a paw at each one just to let them know I mean business. Once past me, they take off running down the lane. I turn and vanish into the swamp and transforming into a songbird. I watch as Zach takes his handkerchief from his pocket and mops his face.

"I don't know where that thing came from, but whoever sent it, I sure thank y'all." He pockets his handkerchief and scratches his head. "That's twice some animal's saved my bacon today. Maybe Mother Nature do love me? No, somethin' funny's goin' on, and I bet Jaqueen knows what's what."

I fly back to the cabin and resume Jaqueen's form just as Zach walks in.

"Hidee Zach. How was school today?"

"You tell me Jaqueen."

"What you mean? How I know 'bout your school day?"

"I just thought you might know 'bout the big dog what bit Darrell this mornin' 'fore he tried ta cut me."

I think I see certainty in his eyes. Can I tell him, Great Spirit?

THAT'S UP TO YOU. IF YOU THINK IT WILL HELP, DO IT.

"Did it look like this?' I transform into a wolf, and he smiles broadly.

"You are some kind o' Mama Loa," he says as I change back

to Jaqueen.

"No, Zach. The Great Spirit has blessed me with the power to become anything I wish. I was sent here by Him to help you. This is my real form."

I transform into my rabbit form and hop on the table.

"Don't let Daddy see you like that. He shoot you for sure." Zach giggles as he covers his mouth with his hand.

I change back to Jaqueen. "You can't tell your Daddy 'bout me, hear?"

"I promise, but now I know how you knows what I does all th' time. You must change into some kind o' insect and follow me 'round."

"That's right. Sometimes I'm a skeeter and sometimes a hawk."

"You buzzed me that day th' cops got us, didn't ya?"

"That was me."

"You gonna stay with us now?"

"You through with Darrell?"

"Yes, Mam, but I think he through with me too. He almos' turn white when he seed you as that big black cat."

"I'll stay around for a while. Least 'till y'all testifies at their trial. The Great Spirit may have some more for me ta do here."

Zach rises from his chair and embraces me. "You th' coolest thing I ever seed, Jaqueen."

I push him away. "You go get busy with y'all's homework. And mind you don't say nothin' 'bout me to yo Daddy."

He releases his hold and smiles at me. "All that's just 'tween you an' me, promise."

He leaves to do his homework, and I get busy with supper.

Chapter 8

The week passes without incident involving Darrell and his buddies. Sunday morning, we head for church, and Zach makes a bee line for Myra. I wish I could transform into a mosquito and listen to their conversations, but I can't leave Moline. When the service ends, Zach rejoins us with a broad smile on his face.

"You look like you heard some good news," I say.

"Sure did. Myra's uncle is the high school basketball coach. She said he told her he'd like to have me on the team, but he didn't want me long as I was tied up with Darrell. She said I should talk to him now that Darrell's out o' my life."

"You gonna do that?" Moline asks.

"You bet. I'm gonna talk ta him right after school tomorrow."

#####

Monday, after Moline leaves for work, I transform into a hawk and fly to the school where I change to a mosquito. I find Zach in a classroom, but I think it's a while before he can talk to the coach. I fly back outside and convert to a hawk again.

Great Spirit, where would I find this 'coach' person?

HE TEACHES ENGLISH DURING THE SCHOOL DAY, BUT HE HAS AN OFFICE IN THE GYMNASIUM. WHY DON'T YOU WAIT IN THERE?

Will you show me the way?

CERTAINLY, GO BACK INSIDE AS A MOSQUITO.

I return to the school, and the Great Spirit guides me to a small office filled with certificates and trophies. I park on the ceiling and wait through several bells before a middle-aged white man with an athletic build and black hair graying at the temples arrives. He takes the chair behind the desk and begins to look at a stack of papers. He leaves his door open, and Zach soon appears. He knocks on the sill, and he coach looks up.

"Come in."

"Coach Landry, I'm Zach Thibodeaux. Your niece said I should talk to you."

Coach Landry looks up from his papers and smiles broadly. "Sit down Thibodeaux. What can I do for you?"

"I'd like ta try out fo' th' team, coach."

"Well, are you finished with Darrell and his gang?"

"Sure am. I don't want no part o' that stuff anymore."

The coach strokes his chin for a moment before speaking again. "I've seen you playing on the schoolyard, and I think you have some talent, but I have to see you against more senior players. Come to practice in an hour, and I'll see how you do with the reserve squad."

"I'll be there coach, thanks for the opportunity."

"Be there a few minutes early and have the team manager give you a uniform, okay"

"I will, thanks again, sir."

Zach leaves the office and paces in the schoolyard impatiently until time for practice. He draws an old uniform from the team locker and suits up with his own shoes. He walks out to the gym floor and approaches the coach who is watching a warm-up drill.

"Here I am, coach."

Coach Landry looks him over and points to the drill. "You know how to do that?" he asks.

"Yes, sir."

"Okay get in behind Jackson there, number 26."

Zach takes his place and executes the drill with precision until the coach blows his whistle. "Okay, I want you boys to meet Zach Thibodeaux," he points to Zach. "Zach's trying to make this team, and I want him tested to the limit. Everybody have a seat except Miller, Stankey, George, Fontenot, Brousard and Zach. We're doing three on three for a few minutes. Stankey, Brousard and Miller, you're one team against the other three. Talk over your assignments and tell me when you're ready.

The teams huddle, and I concentrate on Zach's team.

"You a shooter, Thibodeaux?" Fontenot asks.

"I can shoot okay."

"Good, you can be guard. I'm post and Jack's power forward. They'll double team me any the time I get the ball. Jack here knows to block out so's I can pop the ball out ta you for a shot. I'll do that 'less I got a clear shot on th' inside. You got it?"

"Yeah, I'm ready,' Zach answers.

They break the huddle and turn to the coach. The other team says they're ready, and the coach calls them to center court for a jump ball. Fontenot controls the tip to Zach.

What an interesting game. Do they have to keep bouncing the ball?

IT'S CALLED DRIBBLING, AND THEY MUST DRIBBLE WHEN THEY MOVE. THE OBJECT IS TO GET THE BALL THROUGH THE HOOP. WATCH CAREFULLY.

I watch as Zach 'dribbles' down the floor with one of the other team close in front of him. Can that boy be that close?

YES, HE'S GUARDING ZACH. HE WILL TRY TO TAKE THE
BALL AWAY FROM HIM, BUT HE WILL ALSO TRY TO STOP
HIM FROM PUTTING THE BALL THROUGH THE HOOP.

He keeps slapping at Zach. Is that fair?

ONLY AS LONG AS HE DOESN'T TOUCH HIM.

The other boy jabs at the ball, but Zach changes his 'dribble'
deftly to avoid contact. I marvel at his dexterity. Fontenot calls
for the ball, and Zach makes the ball bounce on the floor and into
his hands. The other boys collapse on Fontenot who passes it
back to Zach while George moves between Zach and the other
players. Zach jumps into the air and launches the ball at the
hoop. It bounces away to an opposing player who begins to run
toward the other end of the floor.

Zach back-pedals to intercept him while the other two boys
take up positions in front of the other hoop. The man in front of
Zach is dribbling and shouting commands to the others of his
team. Zach waits until he takes his eyes off his dribble and swats
the ball away. He dribbles down the floor and leaps into the air
while lifting the ball to the hoop. He puts the ball through the
hoop with one motion and moves back down the floor.

The play continues for several minutes and Zach shoots a few
more times from long range and makes most of the shots until
the other player guards him more closely. Finally, the coach
blows his whistle to stop the play.

"Okay, coach Warren will have practice while I talk to
Thebodeaux. Come with me Zach."

He leads Zach to his office and shuts the door. "Okay,
Thebodeaux, you're on the reserve team. Practice is every
Monday and Thursday after classes from 3:30 to 4:00. I want you

to bulk up some. Spend as much time with the trainer and the weights as you can. I can't guarantee you'll start, that's up to you. I'll give you all the minutes I can, depending on what I see in practice. You start tomorrow."

Zach is beaming from ear to ear as he says, "Thanks coach. You won't be sorry for givin' me a chance."

He shakes the coach's hand and leaves to shower and change. I leave the school and become a hawk for the trip back to the cabin.

Chapter 9

I keep an eye on Zach while he's at school. I don't trust Darrell and his gang to stay afraid of whatever magic they think he has. I do notice Zach spending more time with Myra Le Blanc. I turn into a mosquito to listen in on their conversation during lunch time.

"I made th' team, reserve team, that is."

"I knew you would. My uncle told me 'bout you. He wanted you bad, but he thought you were trouble long as you hung out with Darrell," Myra says.

"I gotta thank my Daddy's cousin for getting' me straight on that score."

Myra looks at him and smiles. "You mean that yella woman with th' big feet and long ears aint his ho?"

"Don't you talk that way 'bout Jaqueen. She a fine lady, and she aint no ho," Zach scolds.

"Well, ever'body think she is. Gator treats her better'n any cousin. Betty Jackson say he buy her some clothes at her Daddy's store th' tother day. Why he do that? I'd think any cousin'd have some clothes with her when she come."

Zach sighs heavily. "Can I trust you t' keep a secret?"

Myra gives him a skeptical look. "What you mean?"

"What I said. Can you keep a secret? Cause what I gonna tell you is a big secret."

She takes on a more serious expression and cocks her head to one side. "You mean Gator gonna marry her?"

"Not that kind o' secret, even bigger'n that."

Myra sits back a bit and crosses her heart. "I swear I'll not tell nobody if'n it's that big."

Zach leans closer to her and whispers. "Jaqueen's some kinda angel, or somethin'."

"What!" Myra shouts. The lunchroom grows silent as all eyes turn on the pair.

"See what you done?" Zach says as he shakes his head in exasperation.

Myra turns to the other students. "It's okay, aint nothin'. Go back t' eatin' y'all."

"I'm sorry, Zach, but I can't believe she's some kinda angel. Why you say that?"

"Cause she is. I don't know, maybe not an angel. I thought she be some kind o' Mama Loa or a witch, but she say she work for the Great Spirit. I guess she mean God, but I don't know. All I know is she got magic powers like a angel or a witch. She showed me how she can turn inta all kind o' animals and birds. I seen her do it."

Myra cocks her head to one side and raises an eyebrow. "You been usin' Darrell's dope?"

"I'm serious, I seen her turn into a wolf an' a rabbit. An' she turn inta a big black cat to protect me from Darrell and his buddies. She say she here t' help me get straight."

She shakes her head in disbelief. "That the strangest thing I ever heard. I guess I gotta believe ya, but you gotta excuse me if think you crazy."

"You gotta promise me you won't tell nobody 'bout this. I promised Jaqueen I wouldn't tell nobody, and I wouldn't tell nobody but you 'cause I think you special, Myra. An' I don't want you thinkin' Jaqueen a ho."

At that point, the bell rings to end the lunch period. Myra rises with her tray. "Can I watch you practice today?" she asks.

"I'd like that if coach'll allow it."

"He'll let me watch. See you later, an' I promise t' keep your secret."

*****

l fly back to the cabin as a hawk and wait for Zach. I really want him to have Myra as a girlfriend, and I decide to let her in on my true form as long as she can truly keep a secret. I'll wait a while to see what she does with Zach's story.

When Zach comes home, I don't say anything about Myra. "How was school today?" I ask.

"School was fine, but basketball practice weren't so good."

"Oh, what happened?"

"I got knocked around a lot, and coach say I gotta put on some muscle."

"Didn't he tell you how t' do that?"

"He say I gotta us th' weight room, but I miss my bus if'n I do that."

Here's where it would be nice if I could operate the pickup, but Moline has that at work every day anyway. I remember the high school's not that far from the lake. "What if I picked y'all up with th' airboat?"

"Y'all knows how t' drive th' airboat?"

"I seen your Daddy do it lots o' times."

Zach looks at me in disbelief. "Alright, you show me. Let's go for a ride."

He takes the airboat keys from the rack by the door and tosses them to me. I feel pretty confident about this, but I still pray, don't let me mess this up Great Spirit.

DON'T WORRY. YOU'LL DO FINE.

We walk out to the airboat, and I take the driver's seat while Zach sits in the bow. I know to put the key in what Moline calls the ignition switch and turn it on. I also know which switch starts the engine, and it roars to life on the first crank. The gauges show operation, but I have no idea what they mean. I grasp the control stick and push down on the pedal that makes the engine go faster.

The boat lurches forward, and I relax my pressure on the pedal to make it sound like when Moline operates it and use the stick to turn out onto the lake. We skim along the water, and the cool wind feels good.

Zach yells back at me, "Y'all really do know how t' drive this, don't ya?"

"You know the Great Spirit wouldn't let me go wrong, don't ya?"

He laughs and says, "Go on down South and see if there's a good landin' place close to th' school."

THE TOP INSTRUMENT IS A COMPASS. YOU'RE GOING SOUTH NOW. SEE, THE NEEDLE IS POINTING TO "S". JUST STAY CLOSE TO THE SHORE ON YOUR RIGHT AND ZACH WILL TELL YOU WHERE TO STOP.

We travel for a short while before Zach points to a pier just ahead. I slow down and coast up to it making sure not to crash into it.

"I knows this dock. I can meet ya here after practice. Y'all can pick me up here 'round four thirty, okay?"

I do some mental calculations. Moline doesn't get home until after 5:30. It only took a few minutes to get here. Supper may have to be a bit later, but I think Moline will understand.

"Okay, we better get back. I gotta fix supper."

After we dock back at the cabin, Zach has a confession to make.

"I tol' Myra 'bout you, Jaqueen. That okay?"

"She believe you?"

He hangs his head a bit. "I don't think so. She thought you my Daddy's ho."

I know what that means now, but it doesn't make any difference.

"Tell you what, you bring her to th' dock tomorrow, an' I'll show her the real me."

His eyes light up like lanterns. "Would y'all?"

"I would. She needs ta know you aint crazy."

He throws his arms around me and gives me a big hug. "You a real bro, Jaqueen."

I assume that's a compliment.

*****

The next day, I pull up to the dock and see Zach and Myra waiting for me.

"Hey Zach, hey Myra," I call.

Zach helps Myra into the airboat and she offers her hand to me. "It's a pleasure to meet y'all, Miss Rabbite."

"You too, an' please call me Jaqueen."

They sit down next to each other in the bow, and I pull away. On the way down I picked out a good spot to show Myra my powers. It's up a small creek to a sandbar. We land there and I tell them to stay in the boat. I transform into a heron and fly onto the sandbar.

"See, I tol' ya," Zach shouts.

I walk over to the airboat and test the sand. It's firm enough to support my human body, and I change back to Jaqueen.

Myra's jaw is hanging down to her waist. "What are you?" she asks.

"I don't know what I am, but the Great Spirit has give me the power to be anything I wanna be. I gots to use my power t' help people or I'll lose it an' jus' be a plain ol jack rabbit agin. Like this." I change into my normal shape and jump into the boat.

Myra picks me up and strokes my fur. "How could I ever think somethin' as magical as you could be a ho?"

I jump from her hands to the deck and become Jaqueen again. "Now you know, an' y'all also know not ta tell anybody 'bout this, I hopes."

"You got no worry there. Aint nobody gonna believe me any more'n I believed Zach when he told me," Myra says.

"Now we got this secret ta share," Zach says.

Myra embraces Zach. "You sure must be some kinda special person ta rate this kinda 'tention from God."

"I allays heard th' preacher say, 'God watches over us', but I never thought he paid me no 'tention. Now I knows it's like th' old hymn says, 'His eye is on the sparrow'," Zach says.

"I been a believer since I was a little girl, but now I knows it's all true," Myra says.

"We rabbits never thought much 'bout th' Great Spirit. Fact, I don't know any animal what does. You humans got a good thing goin' for y'all. You think you know 'bout th' Great Spirit. Y'all call it God, an' most of ya believes even if y'all aint never talked to it. I 'magine some of y'all don't think it's even real. I guess I'm a lucky rabbit 'cause I gets ta talk to it. I can ask it for help, an' it helps me. Seems like it's a good kinda thing, and I 'spects it'd help most anybody what asks with a good heart."

Myra moves from Zach and embraces me. "Jaqueen, you may only be a rabbit, but y'all gotta be givin' me th' best sermon I ever heared."

Chapter 10

It's raining the day of Darrell's trial. Moline and Zach put on their Sunday clothes, and I dress in my best outfit of blouse and jeans. I don't think my Sunday dress is right for the occasion.

I marvel at the sight of the parish courthouse. What a huge building just to punish one kid. I remark about it to Moline.

"My, my what a grand place," I say.

"Don't pay it no mind," Moline says, "Just a big buildin' full o' politicians an' bureaucrats livin' off'n my taxes."

I don't understand why he would have to support such a structure, but the Great Spirit speaks to me.

HUMANS ELECT OTHER HUMANS TO GOVERN THEM. THERE ARE MANY OFFICES IN THAT BUILDING WHERE THE HUMANS WORK WHO TAKE CARE OF THINGS LIKE THE POLICE. YOU'VE SEEN THEM. THEY ALSO HAVE PEOPLE CALLED FIREMEN WHO COME TO HELP YOU IF YOUR HOUSE IS ON FIRE. THERE ARE PEOPLE WHO TAKE CARE OF THE STREETS AND ROADS, AND THIS IS WHERE THE COURTS ARE.

Is that where we're going, to a 'court'?

YES, I'LL EXPLAIN THE ROOM WHEN YOU GET THERE.

We enter the building, and Moline consults a list on one wall to find the courtroom. We go up some stairs and enter a very large room with few windows.

THE WOOD RAIL YOU SEE DIVIDES THE ROOM INTO THE ACTUAL COURT AND THE SPECTATOR SECTION. YOU WILL NOTICE THE RAISED SECTION IN THE MIDDLE. THAT'S WHERE A HUMAN THEY CALL A JUDGE SITS. THE BOX ON THE LEFT WITH THE BENCHES IS FOR THE JURY. A JURY IS COMPOSED OF HUMANS WHO DECIDE THE GUILT OR INNOCENCE OF THE HUMAN ON TRIAL. SINCE THE BOYS ARE NOT ADULTS, THERE WILL BE NO JURY. THE JUDGE WILL DECIDE THEIR CASE.

It's all so impressive. Humans sure do things up big.

I see Darrell, Leeroy and Achmed seated at a table in front of the long wooden rail. The man with them is the lawyer I saw at the convenience store. Two white men and a woman are seated at a table on the other side of the space in front of the rail.

A uniformed man enters the room and calls, "All rise for Judge Landers."

THAT HUMAN IS CALLED A BAILLIF.

Everyone else stands, so I do too. A woman in a dark robe enters from behind the large, raised area and takes a seat. The same man calls, "Be seated." Everyone sits including me.

The judge asks each table if they are ready, and they both answer, "Yes, your honor."

I thought she was a judge. Why do they call her 'honor'?

HUMANS REFER TO JUDGES AS 'YOUR HONOR'.

The judge tells the prosecution to proceed, and one of the white men stands.

"Your honor the prosecution calls Mr. Lyle Aldridge."

The convenience store manager rises and moves to the front

of the room. I notice his right arm is in a sling. The Baillif walks to him with a book in his hand and holds it out toward him. The manager places his left hand on the book, and the officer intones, "Do you solemnly swear that the evidence you are about to give is the truth, the whole truth and nothing but the truth, so help you God?"

The manager repeats, "So help me God."

"State your name."

"Lyle B. Aldridge."

"You may be seated."

The manager takes a chair beside the judge's place but much lower down.

The man they called the 'prosecutor' moves to the manager.

"Are you the manager of the convenience store at 3679 Iberia Street?"

"Yes."

"Please tell the court what happened at your store on October 21st of this year."

"Well, these four black kids came into the store and started shoplifting. I tried to stop them when one of them pulled a gun on me and shot me in the arm. My cashier grabbed the shotgun we keep under the counter and shot back at the kid, but she missed him. He shot at me again then ran out the door."

"Are any of those children in the courtroom now?"

"Yes, sir. Those three at the table there and that tall one sittin' back there." He points to Darrell and his gang then to Zach.

"And what did they steal?"

"They took four packages of potato chips and a six pack of beer."

"That's all I have, your honor. Your witness counselor."

The lawyer for the boys rises. "No questions at this time, your honor."

Aldridge leaves the chair and sits back down in the spectator section.

"The prosecution calls Miss Dora Cunningham."

The Baillif swears her in, and the prosecutor begins.

"Were you present at the convenience store on Iberia Street on the day in question?"

"Yes, I was."

"Did you fire a shotgun at any of the defendants?"

"I fired at that one after he shot Mr. Aldridge." She points to Darrell. "But I missed him."

"That's all I have for now. Your witness."

The boy's lawyer rises. "No questions at this time, your honor."

She steps down, and the prosecutor calls for Zach. Zach walks to the front and is sworn in.

"Were you with the defendants on the day in question?"

"Yes, sir, I was."

"What is your relationship to the defendants?"

"We all go to Franklin High School."

"Did the defendants tell you what they planned to do at the convenience store?"

"Yes, sir. They was plannin' ta steal some stuff to get even with the manager for callin' the cops on us th' last time."

"Did you know Mr. Hebert was armed?"

"No, sir. I thought they'd taken away his gun th' last time. I was surprised when he had it."

"Tell the court what you saw on that day."

"Well, th' bros took some stuff an' started ta leave when the manager..."

The prosecutor breaks in, "You mean Mr. Aldridge?"

"Yes, sir, Mr. Aldridge. He tried ta stop 'em. Darrell pulled out a gun and shot at Mr. Aldridge. I got bit by a skeeter on my ankle and stooped down ta swat it when that shotgun fired and hit the shelf where my head woulda been. Then Darrell and the other guys ran out to th' car an' took off."

Thank you, Mr. Thibodeaux. Your witness."

The boy's lawyer walks up to Zach. "Zach, may I call you Zach?"

"Sure, Mr. Guidry."

"Did you see Miss Cunningham with the shotgun?"

"No, sir. I was on 'tother side o' some shelves."

"So you couldn't see her pointing the shotgun at Mr. Hebert?"

"Well, no, but I heared th' shots."

"Zach, you say a mosquito bit you before the shots were fired?"

"No, sir. After Darrell shot."

"Are you sure you didn't hear a shotgun fired before Darrell fired?"

"I knows th' difference 'tween the sound of a shotgun an' a pistol, sir."

"But you could not see Miss Cunningham pointing the shotgun at Mr. Hebert|?"

"No, sir."

"No more questions, your honor."

Zach came back to his seat, and I could smell the nervous perspiration. Moline leaned next to him and whispered, "You did good, son. I'm proud o' you."

I patted Zach's leg and smiled at him.

The prosecutor says, "The prosecution rests, your honor."

The judge asks, "Are you ready to proceed, Mr. Guidry?"

"Yes, your honor. I would like to recall Cunningham.

She goes to the witness chair and is reminded she's still under oath.

"Miss Cunningham, you said you fired at Mr. Hebert after he fired at Mr. Aldridge. Is that correct?'

"Yes, sir.'

"Before you fired, were you pointing the shotgun at Mr. Hebert?"

"I don't think so. It was all happenin' so fast. I can't be sure."

"Thank you, you may step down.

Mr. Guidry turns to his table. "I call Darrell Hebert."

Darrell takes the stand and is sworn in.

"Darrell, tell us what happened on the day in question," Guidry asks.

"I admits we was shopliftin', but that's all we was doin' when Mr. Aldridge jumps over th' counter an' yells at us, an' that lady point a shotgun at me. I was scared she was gonna kill me, so I takes out my gun and shoots so's ta miss her, but I accidently shoots Mr. Aldridge." Darrell looks straight at Mr. Aldridge, "I's truly sorry fo' shootin' you, sir. I din't mean ta hurt nobody."

"No more questions, your honor," Guidry says.

The prosecutor rises. "Mr. Hebert, why were you carrying that gun?"

"We got attacked by a big dog th' otha day, an' I got it fo' protecshun."

"Were you not told by the police it was illegal for you to carry a firearm the last time you were arrested?"

"Yassuh, but my Daddy say it okay if'n I gets attached by

some big dog to shoot it, an' we was attacked by a big dog tother day. I was scared that dog might go fo' me again."

"No more questions, your honor," the prosecutor sits down.

"The defense rests, your honor," Guidry says.

The prosecutor sums up his case, and Mr. Guidry stands.

"Your honor. These boys are all good students who made some mistakes. They have confessed to shoplifting and will pay the fines associated with that offense. Mr. Hebert has apologized to Mr. Aldridge. We cannot deny Mr. Hebert was in violation of Louisiana law by possessing a firearm, but we ask your mercy in passing sentence on him. Thank you."

The judge consults some papers and says, "Mr. Barnes and Mr. Jackson you are convicted of shoplifting and will pay a $500 fine as well as paying for the items you shoplifted, and you are dismissed. Mr. Hebert, you were given leniency on your first offense of illegal possession of a firearm. I cannot exercise that same leniency in this case as it is your second offense and resulted in injury. I find you guilty of unlawful possession of a firearm and assault with a deadly weapon. I sentence you to two years in juvenile detention." She bangs a wooden hammer on the desk and says, "Court is adjourned."

Chapter 11

Moline takes me to Zach's ballgames, and explains the game to me with a large degree of patience. I think it's thrilling to see Zach score so far away from the hoop. The skill of those boys is truly amazing. Zach doesn't start the first few games, but he quickly earns a starting position.

Myra LeBlanc sits with us sometimes, but she often sits with her girlfriends, embarrassing them by yelling encouragement to Zach.

Back at the cabin, Zach is worn out and drops into bed as soon as he can. Moline goes to the kitchen and opens a can of beer, handing me a soda.

He sits down at the kitchen table, and I join him.

"You must be real proud o' your son," I say.

"You had a big part in straightenin' him out, and he sure thinks th' world o' you."

"We gotta make sure he gets ta go ta college."

"I been lookin' in ta that. Th' university up at Lafayette aint too expensive. If'n I saves my gator money an' takes on a night job, I think I can afford it."

"Don't forget, he might get a scholarship fo playin' basketball," I add.

"That'd be good, but I can't count on that."

"Well, maybe sometin'll come along," I say.

I don't know why I say that, but somehow, I know it will all work out. We finish our drinks and head for bed.

*****

The mailbox for the cabin is up at the highway. Moline gets the mail when he comes home from work. One day, he's busy opening the bills and letters at the kitchen table when his eyes light up with a glow of surprise and wonder.

"Well I'll be darned," he says.

"What is it?" I say.

"There's some TV people what wants ta make TV show 'bout people what hunts gators, an' they wants me ta be on it."

Is that good?

IT MEANS HE'LL HAVE PLENTY OF MONEY FOR ZACH'S COLLEGE.

You did this, didn't you?

LET'S JUST SAY IT'S A LUCKY COINCIDENCE.

"They gonna pay y'all fo that?"

"They don't say nothin' 'bout no money. They just wants to interview me next week."

"I think y'all better do that." I call Zach in from his bedroom doing homework. "Come in here, Zach. Yo Daddy's gonna be on TV."

Zach comes running into the kitchen. "That true, Daddy?"

"It aint final yet. I gotta talk to those TV folks next week. They may not want me."

"Course they'll want y'all," I say. "You good-lookin' 'nuff for TV."

"An' you th' best gator hunter in Lousiana," Zach adds.

Moline blushes a bit but recovers quickly. "I'm glad you think so, both o' ya, but we'll just wait an' see."

*****

Next week, Moline comes in from his interview with a smile that lights up the room. It's easy to tell he got the job.

"They wants y'all?" I say.

"I can't believe it even now," he says. "They gonna give me more money'n I ever thought poss'ble jus' fo' showin' me catchin' gators. College gonna be no problem now."

"Zach'll be so happy," I say as I embrace Moline.

He pushes me back to arm's length. "I know 'bout Zach. I wants ta know 'bout you."

I turn my head away. "What you mean?"

Moline leans closer to me and becomes very serious. "There's somethin' I wanna ask y'all."

"What's that?'

"I don't know quite how ta say this. I aint said it to no other woman 'cept my dear departed Wanda."

I know what he's going to say, and I have to think of some way of letting him down easy.

"It hard fo me to say this, but I wants ya ta marry me, Jaqueen. I knows Zach'd like you fo a mama, an' he needs y'all."

I sit down at the kitchen table and smile at his embarrassment. He sits down opposite me. I reach across the table and take both of his hands in mine. "That's very sweet o' y'all, Moline. I's honored you'd ask me, but I can't marry nobody, an' Zach's got his head on straight now, an' I gots ta leave pretty soon."

"Leave? Where you goin?"

He seems genuinely surprised to hear me say that. His eyes plead with me as much as any words. "I don't care if'n ya marries me, but please stay fo Zach's sake."

I THINK IT'S TIME FOR YOU TO GO NOW. YOUR
ASSIGNMENT HERE IS COMPLETE.

"I'd love ta stay, but I can't. Jus' believe it got nothin' ta do
with how I feels 'bout you and Zach."

"You need some money? I aint got much, but I can give y'all
some."

"No, I don't need no money ta get where I gotta go."

He takes on a serious expression and grips my hands even
tighter. "Y'all scares me with that kinda talk, Jaqueen. What you
mean?"

I'm afraid I've frightened him. I need to give him a rational
explanation for me leaving.

"All that's taken care of. While you was at work, I called my
uncle Moses in Texas. He know 'bout my problems here in
Lousiana, an' he say I welcome ta live with his fam'ly. He a nice
man, an' I al'ays love him more'n any o' my relations."

"Well, I guess you gotta go. When you leavin'?"

"Not 'til I says goodbye ta Zach. I'll tell him t'nite an' leave
in th' mornin'."

"We's sure gonna miss y'all. I'll give ya a ride ta th' bus
station."

No, he won't, but I can't tell him that, and he'd never believe
the real story.

"That's nice o' you, Moline."

Zach comes in from school and starts for his room after a brief
greeting. Moline calls to him, but I say, "It's okay, Zach. You do
your homework. We'll talk after supper."

I fix my fried chicken and all the fixin's that night. After the
dishes are done, I ask Zach to walk with me outside.

We walk along the lakeshore for a while before Zach says,

"What's wrong, Jaqueen?"

"The Great Spirit says I'm finished here, and I gotta go."

He stops walking and turns to me. "Oh, no. I was hopin' you an' Daddy'd get together an' you'd stay."

"You know I can't do that. You know what I really am. Do it make any sense fo' me ta stay?"

He shakes his head and lowers his chin to his chest. "No, it don't, but I sure wish it did."

"You a good boy, Zach. You gonna have a good future. You can be a astronaut now if'n y'all wants."

"Can I write to y'all, Jaqueen?"

"No, I don't get no letters, but if y'all prays to th' Great Spirit, It'll let me know 'bout it."

"I'll sure do that." He takes me in his arms and hugs me tightly. "I gonna miss ya somethin' awful."

I push him away gently. "You jus' 'member all what's happened since I came, an' you take good care o' that LeBlanc gal, hear?"

"Don't worry 'bout that. She gonna be my woman someday."

We walk back to the cabin and go to bed.

Chapter 12

That night the Great Spirit takes me back to my Texas home. It's good to be a rabbit again. I much prefer my fur to clothes, and clover to chicken. I don't have to worry about showering or using that contraption they call a toilet again. I wonder what the Great Spirit will send me to next, but I resolve to enjoy rabbithood until it's time.

*****

Moline is cooking breakfast when Zach comes into the kitchen the next morning.

"How many eggs you want?" he asks.

"Where Jaqueen?" Zach asks.

"She gone in th' night sometime, I guess."

"Oh, yeah. Jus' two scrambled, Daddy." He sits down and drinks his orange juice before Moline sets a plate with eggs, limp bacon and things that resemble biscuits in front of him. Zach stares at his plate and says, "We sure gonna miss her cookin'."

Moline sits down at the kitchen table and sighs heavily. "That a fact."

Zach smiles as he lifts a fork full of eggs to his mouth. He follows it up with a crunchy biscuit before answering. "You hear her leave last night?"

"Not a sound. I don't know how she plan ta get to th' bus station. 'Sides, she leave all o' her clothes here."

"All of 'em?"

"Ev'ry stitch. She had ta go out buck naked, I guess."

Zach chews on a piece of bacon for a while and thinks of how Jaqueen might have changed to leave the lakeside.

"Well Daddy, I aint never seen Jaqueen with no clothes on, but I 'magine she as pretty as a Blue Heron without 'em."

THE END

Acknowledgements

The Jack Rabbit concept is the brainstorm of several brilliant individuals with in our publishing environment.

Bruce Moran
Larry Cavanagh
Jeff and Jacki Lovell
Bob Doerr
Linda and Don Brewer
Jessica and Corby Tate
James Thompson
Each of our fantastic Jack Rabbit Fiction Team Writers.

Join me for another
White Glove Fiction adventure
staring Jack Rabbit

www.ingramcontent.com/pod-product-compliance
Lightning Source LLC
Chambersburg PA
CBHW050459110726
47899CB00003B/999